Back in Charge

Back in Charge

Mariah Greene

LIBRIS

An *X Libris* Book

First published by X Libris in 1995

Copyright © Mariah Greene 1995

The moral right of the author has been asserted

A CIP catalogue for this book
is available from the British Library

ISBN 0 7515 1276 1

Photoset in North Wales by
Derek Doyle & Associates, Mold, Clwyd
Printed and bound in Great Britain by
Clays Ltd, St Ives plc

X Libris
A Division of
Little, Brown and Company (UK)
Brettenham House
Lancaster Place
London WC2E 7EN

Chapter One

ANDREA KING LEANED against the door-frame of the office and wondered how things had ended up this way.

She had made her way through the large open plan office, conscious of eyes upon her. She was aware of others and of herself, even more acutely than normal. She marched smartly out of the lift and picked up speed as she rounded the corner to Martin Cox's office, the windrush almost lifting the tails of her jacket. She needn't have rushed; this was not the sort of meeting where it mattered if she was late.

Tall and sleek, she knew she cut an impressive figure around the offices of DRA. Today was no exception. The clean lines of her features were softened by the gentle cut of a Liz Claiborne suit. Carrying her soft leather briefcase with one hand, she used the other to sweep her light-brown hair away from her face and over her shoulders. Her eyes were delicate brown ovals set into an angled, although not angular, face. Her cheekbones were high and proud, accentuating a neat, straight nose, and she was able to mould her tender lips into the warmest of smiles.

1

Somebody had once described her as second-glance beautiful. They had meant she was able to turn a head just enough to draw a second, more rewarding glance. Once she had that second glance, Andrea had them.

Andrea King was able to carry herself and a situation with ease. Clothes fitted well on her body, her narrow hips and good shoulders supporting full breasts, conveying an effect of poise and confidence. And it was more than just an effect. Sharp clothes and looks were matched by an even sharper brain. Her instincts for a deal and the ability to close a transaction had been the engine that drove her success in the world of advertising.

The office of Carl Anderson, volatile head of the agency and the A in DRA, was empty. As far as the current situation was concerned, his work had been done. Deakin and Richards, the DR part of the act, had long since departed, selling out to Carl Anderson and leaving their initials behind them as part of the deal. Carl Anderson had been able to buy their very identities.

At twenty-nine, Andrea's career with DRA had been impressive. She had worked in several agencies before landing a job as an account handler with DRA. Martin Cox had recruited her. Hard work, determination and a few breaks meant she had unofficially risen in the almost invisible power structure of DRA. She looked after two other new account handlers who would come to her for advice. She ran several key accounts that earned money for DRA – and herself.

Now, things were about to change.

She leaned against the door of Martin Cox's office and thought about the things that had led her there. What had started the chain of events? Was there a single, exact moment that she could fix on? Something that would explain things and make sense of the situation? It was like a rollercoaster ride which had built up slowly before it reached the crest and shot swiftly and heavily downward. The thoughts in her mind ordered themselves and the beginning came to her. And the end.

Like most things, it started and ended with sex.

'Andrea!'

Martin Cox, for probably the fiftieth time in this their first fuck, had called her name into her ear as he pounded away on top of her. She gripped his rear and pulled him to her, the shape of his cock impressing itself inside of her. She raked her nails over his back and squeezed his hips with her thighs. Martin had his arms under her shoulders, supporting himself on his elbows, and his head was buried into her collar bone.

An hour or so earlier, they had been in a bar in Soho, drinking together after a dinner meeting with clients. The clients had gone off in search of flesh in the arid depths of Soho. Martin and Andrea had chosen to seek theirs closer to home. Their conversation had drifted and wandered and Andrea felt sex looming on the horizon. Martin had interviewed her when she first joined the agency almost four years earlier. She had known, from that very first encounter, that he was interested in her. She had made a resolution, also at that very first encounter, that whatever she did in DRA, however successful she was, it would not be the result of fucking Martin. That evening, however, she was curious about him and in the right sort of mood. The way they had ended up in

3

a taxi on their way back to her flat had been virtually wordless.

'Andrea!' again.

She gripped the hair at the back of his head and pulled so she could see his face. It was flushed and covered in sweat, his slightly-too-long black hair clinging to his swarthy skin. His eyes were scrunched into a squint and she had to give his hair another tug before he would open them. She kissed him and then pushed his head back down into her shoulder. She felt her orgasm not far off and wondered if it was rude to come before your boss? Should she even come at all? Of course you should, Andrea, she told herself. Martin would surely think it was important and she certainly did, regardless of Martin. She may even embellish it with a little more noise than usual.

By the time they had arrived at her flat, Martin had used the taxi journey to tell her how much he had always admired her, in every sense. That she was the most – or had he said one of the most? – beautiful women he had ever worked with. And he had worked with many. Tentatively, he had taken her hand and held it. In the flat, when she made a grab for him, the desire suddenly spilling into action, he had looked genuinely surprised, as though he may really have thought they were just going to have coffee. She would have been happy for him to take the lead, but it did not seem that things were going to work out that way. If she had left it to Martin, they would probably be on their tenth cup of coffee by that time.

'Andrea!'

He called her name with a hoarseness that, in the space of fifty or so repetitions, sounded unfamiliar. She suspected he was about to come. His thrusting became more erratic and fevered.

4

The sensation of his body, plastered against hers and glued by sweat, the sounds he was making and the feeling he was giving her as he thrust into her pussy, all combined into a hand that gave her the gentlest of pushes over the edge.

Their orgasms were synchronised to each other in a way that could only be beginner's luck. She held him tight inside of her, contracting around him as he pulsed his come into her. Cool waves of pleasure lapped at her body and the intensity of the sex was pushed through a small gap in their senses before subsiding into a peaceful feeling. His cock quivered in her and she felt the tingle where he had rubbed against her.

'Andrea!'

Two and a half months later, she had lost count of the times he had called her name in this way.

She pressed her hands on to his shoulders, pinning him to the bed. She gyrated her hips, grinding herself on to him. She juddered as she stimulated him with her vagina. He grunted and squinted, the familiar flush covering his face. She rode him as he came in heated, fitful bursts.

For a few moments she stayed sitting on his prostrate body. He opened his eyes and looked at her.

'What about you?' he asked her.

'Oh, I'm done,' she said looking at him and wondering if he knew what she really meant.

'Andrea!'

'Martin, if you're going to shout, I'll put this phone down. Don't be embarrassing.'

Andrea turned her pen over in her hand, underlining something in her daybook that she must remind Tim about.

'I'm not shouting, Andie,' he said to her.

'Martin, please don't call me Andie. I'm not here to feed some Hollywood fuck-fantasy for you. I have a call to make and we both have to be away for the MCC course, so now is not the time for this conversation.'

One of the junior planners, Tim Matthews, wandered past the glass partition of her office. He looked in at her through the Venetian blinds which were partially open. She motioned for him to come in and wrote something on a Post-It note as he made his way to her desk. She handed it to him and looked skyward. He smiled at her. She watched him as he left, her mind distracted from Martin on the other end of the line.

'. . . and then just tell me it's over,' was all she heard of his sentence, although she caught the gist of it.

'Martin. I had fun. You had fun. We had fun.' She made the sentences short and clichéd in the hope that the message would be clear, that the logic of it would be apparent. Their dalliance was over. 'Now it's time to move on. There doesn't have to be any bad feeling here.'

'Andrea, I . . .'

'Martin, I've got a call waiting here,' she lied. 'Let's talk later, at the hotel, okay?'

MCC was the Management Communication Course that DRA insisted all people at her level should be sent on. It consisted of three modules, two days each, spread over a period of nine to twelve weeks. Despite DRA's insistence that it was a benevolent, growth experience for all concerned, Andrea was convinced they used it as a way to weed out people they did not like and to select those who would be groomed for greatness.

In the great scheme of who was being groomed,

Andrea had felt confident. Her work was good and all her accounts raved about her. She was ready to move to the next level. So many times, she looked at what went on in the agency around her and was frustrated by it. She could see ways that things could be done better, more efficiently for everyone, clients included. She understood the bigger picture and what went towards its composition. In the hyper-hyper world of advertising, with its paranoia and porcelain egos, Andrea was able to see above it and understand what made the business tick. In her current position, however, she was on a largely self-contained track, like almost everyone in DRA. It was the way Carl Anderson liked it. Andrea's feet had begun to itch in the past months and she felt inside herself that she would give it another six months before she forced the issue. Still, she knew she was a prime contender.

And then Gillian Kay had come along. More precisely, she had come along again. Andrea knew her of old. From her earliest days in advertising. Five years earlier they had worked together at the first agency where Andrea had landed a serious job. A little younger and a bit more impressionable, Andrea had been carried along on the wave of Gillian's smooth talk. Gillian could turn it on when she had to. It was Andrea's induction into agency politics and she was horrified when she saw her hard work and ideas being paraded as Gillian's own. That was five years ago. Even at the time, still relatively inexperienced, Andrea knew that making a public fuss was not the right thing to do. It was better to bide time and get even when the time was right. When Gillian reappeared at DRA, Andrea realised that during her own swift rise through the ranks of advertising, she had not completely forgotten about her score with Gillian. And now she was more equipped to deal with it.

Gillian was out of scale to everyone else in all ways. Her personality just a bit too domineering, her features a little big, her dress sense just not quite right. But despite or because of all this, Gillian Kay was a formidable force and she had been brought into DRA six months earlier. Rumours abounded about how much they had head-hunted her for, what package she was on, what she had done with Carl Anderson to get the job. The usual rumour mill.

To Andrea, it was more serious than simply a source of gossip. Martin had said at the time that Gillian Kay was being brought in on an equal footing with her, that they would be able to work together. He had given her some clichéd speech about the friction giving off creative sparks between them. She had told him flatly that Gillian Kay was a scheming bitch and she did not trust her. She told Martin he should not trust her.

In retrospect, she wondered if she hadn't started sleeping with Martin as a way of trying to neutralise the threat Gillian Kay represented. Gillian at thirty-two was three years older than her and would seem an obvious choice for a senior position. That must be why she moved, thought Andrea. Whatever Andrea's own motives had been, sleeping with Martin for nearly ten weeks had been a miscalculation. Cutting him off the way she had would cause a few problems but, in the long run, a clean break was going to be best.

'Do you want me to fax the research figures to the hotel for you?'

She looked up. It was Tim. Nineteen, short hair,

tall and enthusiastic. He was keen to get on and keen to please Andrea. She had seen that kind of shoot-for-the-stars enthusiasm in so many people, herself included, and she saw what happened when it got dampened. She hoped that would not happen with Tim.

'That'd be great. I'll be there from about eight-thirty this evening. I'll look it over tonight. I'll give you a call tomorrow assuming we get a break on the course, unless they have some sort of sensory deprivation exercises planned.'

'Maybe you'll do a case study of Gillian Kay,' he smiled at her. She knew he was always ready to feed her lines about Gillian.

'We'd need more than two days, Tim. It will be interesting to see how Ms Kay copes with the rigours of self-exploration.'

The MCC course had taken on a folklore of its own around DRA and it was seen by many as an indoctrination procedure. One of Andrea's previous bosses had come back and been like an evangelist for the first few weeks before slipping back into her old ways.

'What sort of things do you do on the course?'

'It's difficult to tell. It's like all of those sort of courses, they like to keep you guessing. I've done ones in the past, so I know a bit of what to expect.'

He was standing in front of her desk. Their conversations were limited to the amount of time he could usefully stand in front of her and chat. If she had time, she would occasionally motion for him to sit down. He was trained enough by now to know that you did not sit unless asked. She would have liked to have talked with him but she didn't have time. Their standard period of friendly silence indicated that the conversation was over.

'I'll fax them tonight, then,' he said, leaving.

9

Chapter Two

'*MAKE IT A* large one,' smiled Andrea at the barman, her face more sweet than she felt.

Martin's presentation on the MCC course, almost nine hours ago now, still lingered in her mind as one of the most tedious experiences of her recent life. She needed to shake the feeling. She cringed at the thought that she'd actually been out with Martin, listened voluntarily to his drone. Worse, she'd fucked him, and he was no more interesting naked.

Idly, she let her eyes travel from the empty glass and on up to the optics where the barman reached to put a large measure of gin into a tall, straight glass. He was well built with square shoulders, and hair she would have considered too long for his job. While his shoulders were wide, his hips were narrow and looked easily grabbable. He would have been in his late twenties, perhaps even his early thirties. A mite too old to be pulling pints in a hotel bar, but she was not complaining. Andrea shifted on the barstool, an unsettled feeling between her legs.

She was drained. Two more modules of the course left. There were no great surprises. Just the usual management philosophy, rôle-playing, self- and other-evaluation. She'd been there before. Gillian Kay had seemed nervous when she introduced herself to the rest of the group. They had been instructed not to talk about work in the introduction. Andrea suspected it was an attempt to humanise themselves to each other, to show they had lives outside. It pleased her to realise that Gillian did not. Andrea made sure she complimented Gillian on the succinctness of her introduction.

She was on top of the situation at work, she knew, but still her mind was filled with thoughts; about Martin, about the course and about Gillian Kay. Right from the start, when she'd been told Gillian was being brought in to the agency, Andrea knew there was a potential problem. She would have to watch her back. Gillian Kay might be a threat, but so can you, Andrea, she told herself.

The barman eyed her appreciatively – and not for the first time – as he set down a paper coaster and the glass on top of it. She signed the bar receipt, then looked at him and studied his badge. She smiled when she read it. The barman looked at her questioningly, as though wrongly accused of something, his face like a cheeky boy.

'Sorry,' she said. 'I thought it said Martin, not Michael.'

'Most people call me Mike, but the hotel won't allow it on our badges.' He raised his eyes.

'Which do you prefer? Michael or Mike?'

'I don't mind, tell you the truth,' he said. His accent had a faint trace of the Midlands that had been almost eradicated by too long in a hotel in the home counties. 'You've been here before, haven't you?'

'My company uses the hotel for courses, conferences, that sort of thing.'

There was a moment of finely balanced silence between them, where it seemed that many hasty and private calculations were being made in Michael's mind. She wondered what they might be. She did not have to think too hard, as she had a fair impression of what was on his mind. By barely an inch, she opened her legs on the stool and leaned forward on to the bar.

'Is the bar open all night?' she asked.

'No. We're supposed to close it at midnight,' he replied, polishing a glass. 'The Piano Bar opens late and then there's the night porter.'

She drew a quick, silent breath before speaking.

'This may seem a bit forward, but I'm in room 316 and if you're finishing shortly, perhaps you'd care to come along for a drink.'

Surprise registered in Mike's eyes and Andrea watched as he pretended to be cool, the glass in his hand suddenly receiving a more frantic polish. His lips pursed and then relaxed.

'My name's Andrea, by the way,' she said, standing and ignoring the drink on the bar as she marched smartly out.

Up in her room she tidied a loose pair of knickers and a stray blouse into her overnight bag before pushing it into the wardrobe. The double bed had been turned down for the night. Whilst eating the chocolate mint from the pillow, she pulled at the covers, removing all of them except the white undersheet. The bed was ready for sex. Square, flat and white with nothing to get in the way and no incentive for him to stay the night. She flicked on the television and found the porn channel. She left the volume low as bodies writhed around in

12

different positions on the screen.

In the bathroom she gave her teeth a brush and looked at herself in the mirror. Giggling at the thought, she considered for a few seconds before hitching up her skirt and pulling off her knickers.

There was a knock at the door. She looked at her watch. Seven minutes past twelve. Not bad, she thought, smiling. She was about to put her knickers into her cosmetics bag when she thought better of it. She held on to them and waited for his second knock. It came. Knickers in hand, she made her way unhurriedly to the door.

'Hello,' she said, looking at him warmly, the heat of her desire suddenly welling in her. She felt her skirt rub against her bared pussy, and it was all she could do to stop herself shoving a hand to the front of her skirt. She composed herself.

'Come on in.' She moved to one side to allow him past.

'I brought this,' he said, 'from the bar,' holding up a bottle of red wine.

He had faltered midway through his sentence as he noticed the bed and the television. He looked around and seemed uncertain where to sit. Andrea sat on the edge of the bed.

'Do you have a corkscrew?' she asked him, the groans of a couple doing it doggie-style playing faintly in the background.

He produced a bottle opener and corkscrew from a chain on his black uniform trousers and looked pleased with himself, like he had pulled a rabbit from a hat. Quickly he uncorked the bottle and went off to the bathroom to get the mouthwash tumblers from the sink.

Andrea watched him as he went. His torso was strong and his legs would be muscular, she could

13

tell. She thought of him in just underwear and then in nothing at all. She looked at the television, a man on top of a woman grunting and grimacing in the heat of fake sex. She was restless, the material of her skirt unfamiliar on her bare bottom.

Mike set the glasses down on the dressing-table and poured.

'Leave those for now,' said Andrea, 'and come over here.'

She reached out and took the chain from his pocket, the one that held the bottle opener, and tugged it gently. He grinned at her. She saw him eye the knickers in her hand. She lifted them so he could see.

'I didn't think I'd be needing these.'

She eyed the bulge in Mike's trousers. On screen, the woman underneath the man cried out as she orgasmed.

Andrea stood and kissed Mike hotly, holding him by the neck. He responded and gripped her tightly, his hands soon running down her back and over her behind. Andrea pulled his shirt out from his trousers and felt the tight flesh on his narrow hips. He did almost the same to her blouse. As she unbuttoned his shirt, so he unbuttoned her blouse. His flies, the zip on her skirt. Like a mirror image of each other, they undressed practically in parallel until Mike was in just a pair of tight blue briefs and Andrea was naked.

Mike's body was firm, with smooth clean lines. A sprouting of hair on his chest caught the glow in the room and looked golden. The line of hair on his stomach stopped abruptly at the hem of his briefs. She looked into his face.

'Tongue me,' she said to him.

Mike knelt in front of her and held her by the tops of her legs, his thumbs pointing inwards as though he were about to peel her open. She saw his eyes light up and watched the tip of his nose get closer to her mons as he homed in. He nuzzled into her pubic hair and she was ready to explode. She wanted him to open her and expose her to him. It would release the steam that was building in her.

She held Mike by the sides of his head and urged him in closer to her. She felt his tongue trace the outside of her lips, their stickiness helping them move almost of their own accord. Like along the edge of a glass, Mike ran his tongue up and down her. She moved her feet further apart on the carpet.

With his thumbs, Mike carefully eased open her pussy lips. It felt as though there was a great windrush, she was so hot. She could feel Mike's breath around the opening of her vagina. He moved himself in closer and she gasped and threw her head back. When she looked down at him, all she could see was the top of his head, as though he were glued to her, a part of her. But she could feel him. His tongue was lapping at her pussy, occasionally pointing itself directly into her hole and at other times lashing on her clitoris with small, whip-like movements.

The damp stickiness had been overcome by a steady stream of juices that washed through her and which, it seemed, Mike would have been content to drown in as he lapped away at her. She wondered if she could possibly drown him, so drenched did she feel.

Each time the tongue flicked her clitoris it sent a wave through her that reverberated up her spine and through her whole body, overloading her, ravishing her senses. Swollen and engorged, her clitoris was the tip on which her desire was focused. She felt the need to release the desire, but felt at a deeper level the desire to be penetrated.

Relentlessly Mike's tongue continued its assault on her. She ground herself against him, running her hands through his hair. Her legs quivered and she felt a spasm in the back of her thighs. Her breath escaped as she dropped her head forward, feeling an orgasm whisper deep inside of her. She was ready to coax that whisper into a shout. She was dizzied, and rested herself on Mike for support as she felt the surge through her body. She was about to come in Mike's face.

She cried out, gripping him harshly on the back of his neck. Closing her eyes she let her neck muscles relax, riding the sensation as best she could in the heat of the moment. Her pussy convulsed and the movement of it was echoed through her whole body. The tense and taut orgasm galloped through her.

Slowly she felt herself at the other side of the orgasm, her breath regulating. Mike had removed himself and was gasping, his hand resting on his knees as he sat back on his ankles. Andrea drank some wine and sat down on the end of the bed, her face almost level with Mike's. She kissed him and then ran her hands over his chest, his pectoral muscles lightly defined. The last of her orgasm rang through her like a distant noise.

'Stand up, Mike,' she said, using his name for the first time.

She removed his blue briefs, freeing his cock, which was well formed and hard. She gripped it lightly, its heat filling her hand as much as its size did. Carefully she eased back his foreskin to reveal the glans, purple and angry.

16

Guiding his cock down she rubbed the tip over her right nipple. She manoeuvred her breast with her free hand so that the point of her nipple would rub the underside of Mike's shaft near the tip. She could feel the heat coming from the whole of Mike's groin area, giving off the signal desire that he wanted to fuck. She did too, but she wanted him even hotter and harder before she was ready to let that happen.

Andrea arched her back so that her breasts stood out more prominently. Mike massaged them with his large hands and she felt herself become pliable in his grip, her mounds moving and shifting with him. She held his cock and pulled it into the cleft between her breasts. Pulling Mike's hands away she replaced them with her own and made a sheath around the shaft with her breasts. She moved herself around the cock, up and down it, bringing the foreskin backwards and forwards. She stopped and was sure she could feel the pulse of his heart through the cock, unless it was her own heart, so near to him in this position.

As she continued to guide him between her breasts, Mike's movements became more urgent and he was practically on tiptoe, trying to set the pace. Still Andrea wanted to wait a little longer. At another time or place, the idea of Mike coming over her breasts would have been attractive. To watch him bring himself off with her mounds, his face as he spurted semen on to her soft flesh. The way she could rub the come around her nipples. But she wanted him inside her. A few more minutes would be enough.

Moving back so that she was lying, but taking Mike with her, Andrea lay on the bed with him straddling her, his cock still between her breasts.

17

His face was imploring.

'Soon,' she said. 'Soon. A bit more first.'

She lay back and watched his tight stomach and shoulders move as he carefully shafted her between her firm breasts. His cock was swollen and distended, pumped up and full. The gentle friction between her breasts created a tingling sensation. She liked the feel of his legs as he straddled her, his hands resting on the bed above her head. His hair fell forward into his face and his look was one of rapt concentration. She held her tits together for a few moments longer and then released them. Mike stopped thrusting.

Raising herself up, Andrea rolled Mike over on to his back. They scooted up the bed as she did so. Her tits and pussy were tingling furiously, her clitoris feeling like a beacon. Mike's cock was rock solid. This time, she straddled him.

She sat on his stomach, then bent forward and kissed him, using her lips to open his and explore with her tongue. For the first time in a while she became conscious of the television. She looked over her shoulder and saw a woman standing against a wall, her head visible over a man's shoulder. She was banged against the wall as he fucked her, her eyes closed as though in ecstasy.

Andrea lifted herself so she was almost completely clear of his body. She was suspended above Mike, looking at his hard naked body, ready for it to penetrate her own and become, for a short time, one with it. She moved her buttocks down his body, using her knees as a lever and she lowered herself against him, feeling his cock come up through her legs as she did so. Mike's shaft was rigid against his stomach and when her pussy was over the underside, she paused. She trailed her lips back and forth over his cock and looked down at the film of fluid she left there. Soon he was oiled up like a bodybuilder.

She held the cock upright, which was not easy, and positioned herself over it. She used the tip to explore her lips and just beyond. She looked at him and then at his cock. She thought of the distance she was from his body at that moment, hanging in the air above the tip of his cock. She thought of the journey she would make down the cock, the way it would fill her, before she would be joined again to Mike. She wanted him in her and up her, to be stretched and filled by him.

The first inch or two of a new cock was always Andrea's favourite and she did not want to rush things. Keeping her legs as far apart as she could so as to widen her pussy, she guided the tip into her. When it was just in, she stopped and sighed, feeling the joy of what was in her and anticipating what was to come. It was as though from the position she was in, straddling Mike with his cock just inside her, she could tell what kind of fuck it would be. The way the cock would slowly fill her, pound at her and finally release itself inside her.

Inch by inch it entered her. She lowered herself delicately and gently, her pussy lips against his shaft, the walls of her vagina expanding blissfully. Eventually she felt his balls against her rear. She reached round and felt them, small and stone-like. He groaned as she tickled them. They held their position and he looked up at her, reaching his hands out to her breasts. She touched his cheek and ran her fingers along his jawbone.

Starting by curving her spine, Andrea leaned back towards Mike's feet at the end of the bed. She felt the front of her thighs stretch as she arched back, her hands now behind her and on Mike's knees. Mike cried out as she leaned further back and her hands found his ankles, which she gripped,

She could feel the odd angle of his cock in her. She wondered if he was enjoying the sight, her splayed pussy with his cock crammed into it. Carefully, Andrea moved herself slightly back off the shaft and then down on to it again. The angle made it feel strange, the majority of the pressure falling against the top of her pussy. She held him and then released him. And then again. She could sense him getting restless so she sat back up and went down on his cock as far as she could, their bodies tightly together.

A hand on each of his shoulders, the ridge of his collar bone against the palms, Andrea began. Almost in time with her breathing she rose and fell on to Mike's cock. Underneath her, his hands either side of his head, Mike's eyes were closed. She held her desire in check with patience, enjoying the feel of the cock up inside of her, the sensation of it being there, not being there and the fervour of the thrust itself.

The noise of the television was slowly drowned out by the noises Andrea and Mike made. At first it was the sounds of their bodies, the physical noise of skin against skin, the only thing between them a lubrication of their juices. As Andrea became more insistent with her lunges on to the shaft, the bed creaked and the sheets rubbed under them. Her breaths became short and more audible, a small cry accompanying each downward movement she made. The insistence of this was punctuated at different intervals by the moans from Mike.

Andrea held him tighter and shimmied up and down him, taking him almost the full way out of her before snatching him back up, his cock rubbing her clit as she did so. It was as though he had disappeared for a second and a moment later was back again, plumbing her depths. Sweat covered them and the sheet grew damp around the borders of Mike's prone body. Inside her she felt a rumbling like distant thunder. Mike groaned and Andrea suspected he was close to coming.

'Just a bit longer. Hang on, Mike. Hold on to it.'

There was nothing left between them now but the rhythm. That was it. The intensity, the depth, the speed and the feel of their two bodies all tuned into a single frequency – the rhythm. All of Andrea was focused between her legs, as though all the energy in her body and every thought in her brain was forcing itself down there. It was the opening through which she would, at any moment, burst and explode. It would eradicate her for a few seconds, taking her somewhere else, a place that she could not describe well but was familiar enough with. She knew how to get there and to make the journey itself enjoyable. At the end of this journey came only rhythm, the beat of herself summed up for brief seconds.

Faster she pushed on to Mike's cock, feeling the orgasm stir in her, making a journey through her. A mixture of moments past and present that culminated in a fluid more potent than any other.

A small sound, almost a weeping, escaped her and she came. She came so deeply and profoundly she ended in a place words could not adequately guide her through. Always the orgasm was a purge, a rush and a release. All her senses flowing in a single direction, the gates and filters in her mind allowing the data to hum and buzz at the precise frequency.

Convulsions racked her and she was lost in herself momentarily, oblivious to the body under her and inside her. She occupied her own private space and enjoyed its intense familiarity.

Mike re-entered her consciousness and she knew he was coming. His cock pulsed in her and he ground his clenched teeth, nostrils flaring. She felt him inside, warm shots touching her. She squirmed over him, accentuating her movements on him as much as possible, almost inflicting his orgasm on him.

They lay on the bed for over twenty minutes, no covers on them, the porn channel still flickering away. She felt his semen move in her and sighed, running her hand over his back and nestling closer into his chest, wanting to shelter in it for a few moments longer. He stroked her and ran his fingertips over her skin, the small charge making her shudder. Gently she drifted into a doze, her mind clean and refreshed.

Suddenly, from nowhere, a thought popped into her brain. Something they had not done for a while now. It would be fun. It might even help her gain some ground on Gillian Kay. It might not, but at least it would be fun.

Now wide awake she sat up and Mike looked at her quizzically as she spoke under her breath.

'A girls' night out.'

Chapter Three

HOTEL SEX. THERE really was nothing like it. Back at her desk, Andrea drifted off, recalling her encounter with Mike in the hotel after the first module of MCC. After Martin's futile attempts at erotic passion in the dying throes of their dalliance, Mike's hard and relentless fucking had brought some well-needed relief. It had set her back on the road. She had remembered, after a short lapse, what it was about sex that kept her looking for more and different kinds of it.

It was just before six in the evening. She redirected her attention back to the campaign brief in front of her. The words floated past her eyes and she tried to anchor them in her mind. She could not. Her thoughts were everywhere. Looking up, she saw Tim Matthews wander past with a box. He had been drafted in to help move some files into archive. Andrea wondered why advertising agencies even needed an archive. It smacked far too much of evidence. Still, papers went into boxes and boxes were stored downstairs until they were taken off site. That, of course, allowed people to come back with the line 'they're archived off site, sorry'.

The DRA building sat on the crease where the City melded into the West End. Office buildings, warehouses and blocks of flats vied with each other in an attempt to establish some semblance of order. From the outside to the inside, DRA looked every bit an agency. Clients expected no more or less from them. Smoked glass, Venetian blinds and potted plants. There were several open plan central areas with offices formed from glass partitions acting as a surround.

The most telling geographical and political fact about DRA was that it did not possess a boardroom as such. There were meeting rooms where clients were presented to and pitched to and where internal meetings were conducted, but there was no boardroom. No star chamber where the future of DRA was thrashed out. Simply, there was no board.

The agency was like a collection of stones thrown into the air. When they landed, four obvious and typical agency groupings formed. Account Executives, Planners, Creatives and Media. In this sense, DRA was not so unusual. Each of these sections had people in overall charge and they met with Carl Anderson on a regular basis to update him, but none of them voted and none of them held any significant proportion of the shares. It was, by one measure, the largest privately held advertising agency in the business.

It was no surprise to Andrea that within DRA, the two people she trusted most were women. She had heard many theories espoused, mostly by men, on the subject of women working together. That they did not get on with each other; that they concerned themselves with issues that men did not; that their menstrual cycles converged into one enormous cyclone of PMT. She had been around long enough to know that like any stereotype, it was important to hold the grain of truth but more important not to be swamped by it. Whoever else she knew in DRA, it was Deanna Clarke and Carol Page she would go to or who would go to her.

In agency terms, they were at different ends of the scale but no less important for it. Carol Page headed up the media section, looking after both the media buyers and the media planners, her own background lodged firmly in the former. She had the most piercing mind Andrea had come across and she demonstrated it with an even sharper tongue. She kept the people who worked for her in check with a combination of fierce wit and the occasional dressing down. Around the agency people said you could fuck Carol Page about – once.

Deanna Clarke was a secretary and in the agency it made her powerful. She looked after Mike Mitchell who in turn tended to the loose bag of art directors, copywriters and sundry free-lancers who laboured, sometimes, under the term 'creatives'. Because DRA had no one in charge of the creative direction outside of Carl Anderson himself, Mike Mitchell's role was ambiguous. Deanna had access to some high-level information and was a favourite of Carl Anderson. She was able to gather the loose strands that fell under Mitchell's brief and pull them into something that made sense. A feat not often accomplished by Mitchell himself.

Every so often, Andrea, Deanna and Carol would get together for a night out. It had been too long since the last get-together and Andrea was looking forward to it. Tonight they had arranged to meet in the wine bar at six-thirty. As usual they would go to Cranes, a small cellar not far from Leicester Square. As a wine bar, it was one of London's best kept secrets, attracting neither tourists nor, what would have been much worse, advertising people. It was run by a woman who reminded Andrea of Joan Collins. She would not have been out of place in a US soap opera. Her image was a heightened sense of fifties glamour repackaged in a nineties sensibility. Carol said she was always waiting for the bevy of young bow-tie clad men who worked there to carry her through the bar while she sang 'Diamonds Are A Girl's Best Friend'.

The walls of Cranes were adorned with dozens of eight-by-ten photographs of celebrities, most of whom had never been there. One or two that had probably never been to England, still less Cranes. None of this mattered. In fact, it served to enhance the effect. They would spend an evening gossiping about people in the office, about their sex lives and about whoever happened to be in Cranes.

By the time she had finished with the campaign brief, Andrea was running late. She called to see if Deanna was still in her office or had left. She must have left already. Carol had an off-site meeting and was going directly to the bar. Andrea gathered her things, sweeping a few papers into her bag, switched off the desk lamp and made her way to the door.

'Night.'

She turned. It was Tim Matthews.

'Are you still here shifting boxes?'

'Yeah, but I'll be off soon.'

'I'll know if you're still wearing the same shirt tomorrow. Night.'

'Night,' he repeated in virtually the same tone of voice.

She watched him as he went in the opposite direction. He was wearing close-fitting cream jeans and a brown waistcoat over a blue shirt. Despite all odds, the ensemble matched. She left and hailed a taxi.

'Evening,' smiled one of the waiters as she entered Cranes. On her journey down the stairs, she had been accompanied by the images of Shirley Bassey, Laurence Olivier, Michael Caine and Anthony Hopkins to name a few. The small entrance hall had a hardwood floor and her heels clicked satisfyingly as she walked.

'Hello,' she said to the waiter.

'Your friend is here already,' he said, smiling.

'Thanks,' Andrea said, spying Deanna and a bottle of wine on the table near the never-used grand piano.

'Sorry I'm late,' she said, settling into one of the heavy chairs. 'See you've got the glasses ready.'

'Of course,' replied Deanna, pouring.

The waiter hovered by the bar, glancing in their direction, the smile still on his face.

'I've had enough of barmen,' said Andrea, letting the sentence hang. She watched as Deanna processed the information.

'What do you mean, And?' she said. Andrea enjoyed Deanna's contraction of her name. It sounded good at the end of sentences, an air of expectation and more to come.

'Let's just say I got involved in a bit of a tussle with a barman at the hotel the other night.'

'What about Martin?' Deanna asked.

'That's over, Deanna.'

Deanna looked at Andrea. Deanna's features

were strong. Her jawbone was square and her cheekbones high. Her hair swept into her face. She was three years younger than Andrea.

'Since when?'

'Since Monday. I would have told you sooner but you know how things are,' said Andrea.

'How's he taking it?'

'At first he was shocked, I think, like it was some sort of slight on his manhood. He seems better now. You know how frightfully decent he can be.'

Deanna nodded and took a sip from her wine.

'God save me from media reps.' It was Carol. In her early forties, devilishly thin and with heavy-framed glasses. Her hair was jet black. 'The only thing worse than a media rep is a sober media rep.'

'Hi,' said Andrea and Deanna almost in unison.

'What did I miss?' asked Carol.

'Well, Andrea shagged a barman the other night when she was away on the course,' said Deanna.

'Obviously,' replied Carol. 'It's part of the course work. Where's Joannie tonight?'

'I've only just got here,' said Andrea.

'I haven't seen her,' said Deanna. 'Just the boys.'

'Her own personal harem. Nice. Guess who called me last night?' said Carol.

They looked at her, waiting.

'Gerry.'

The very name of Carol's ex-husband was enough to send her into vile fits, so it was a shock to hear her say it.

'What did he want?' asked Deanna.

'He has some new girlfriend. She's twenty-three. They're going off to use the place in

Antigua and I think he wanted to ask me if it would be all right. He's scared I'd find out.'

'Twenty-three,' said Andrea.

'I know,' said Carol. 'Mid-life crisis, I feel. I said he should take Jenny as well, they might have a lot in common. They can discuss pop groups. Do each other's hair.'

Jenny was Carol and Gerry's daughter, now seventeen.

'When are you off to Rome, And?'

'Next week. Philip has set up a meeting with Lazzo. They want to run a UK-specific campaign for the aftershave.'

'Shop,' called Carol. 'We're not allowed to discuss that, remember? Mind you, we could discuss Philip.'

'Did Andrea tell you she's dumped Martin, Carol?'

'No. Well done. I thought he looked a bit down today. You're well out of that one.'

'I know,' said Andrea. 'Thanks.'

'What was he like?' asked Deanna.

'Just boring really. That was the worst part. It wasn't even bad sex, it was just boring sex. You always knew what to expect, so it got to the point where it didn't seem worth doing it.'

'Did he do the bit on Anderson's car with you?'

'How do you know about that?'

'I'd like to be able to say that someone told me about it, but unfortunately, I've been there,' said Carol.

Deanna looked on questioningly.

'It was the only faintly exciting thing we ever did,' explained Andrea. 'One afternoon, we went down to the car park and I gave him a blowjob on the bonnet of Anderson's car.'

'Yes, and as I recall, Martin goes from 0 to 60

29

faster than the Porsche,' added Carol.

'Thank God that's all over,' said Andrea.

'I think you've got another admirer in the office,' Deanna said to Andrea.

'Who?'

'Tim Matthews. He was asking me about you today. How long you'd been with the company, things like that.'

'He's a baby, practically,' said Andrea. 'I'd be like Carol's Gerry.'

'Please,' said Carol, 'it's different for girls. Tim's at his peak right now. What better time? I might myself, if you're not interested.'

'I didn't say I wasn't interested,' said Andrea. 'Just that I'd need some time to think about it.'

'Like about five seconds?' said Carol.

'Gillian Kay was having a go at him earlier today. Something about some data she wanted and hadn't received,' said Deanna.

'What's her problem?' said Carol.

'Do you want a list?' said Andrea. 'She's a bitch on wheels. I can't believe we hired her.'

'What's the story with you two, anyway?' Deanna asked Andrea.

'It's a long story, believe me,' interjected Carol.

Andrea drew a breath, thinking about the specific event over five years ago. The way she had felt when Gillian passed off a campaign idea as her own. In some ways, it seemed funny now. Shampoo of all things.

'She is a liar,' Andrea said to both of them. 'I trusted her back when I was just starting out. She took me in, in every sense. Cow.'

'They worked at the same agency,' Carol explained to Deanna, who did not look particularly enlightened by what Andrea had just said. 'Gillian lifted some of Andrea's ideas. Not just a

30

little light plagiarism, like we all do from time to time, but wholesale theft.'

'Didn't you do anything about it?' Carol asked.

'Not yet,' said Andrea.

Carol called a waiter over and they ordered another bottle of wine.

'Don't worry about her all the time, Andrea,' said Carol. 'She's all Bill Amberg and no knickers. There's no substance there and that'll show through eventually.'

'She was in her office listening to self-hypnosis tapes today,' said Deanna.

'Which ones?' asked Carol.

'Self-esteem, I think.'

'You can buy self-hypnosis tapes for natural breast enlargement,' said Carol.

'How to get ahead in advertising, you mean?' said Andrea.

'How to give head in advertising,' amended Deanna.

'Three months I've been listening to them,' Carol said, lifting her breasts, 'I want a refund.'

Like many things Carol said, Andrea was never quite sure if they were true or simply Carol being devilish for the sake of it.

'I'm serious,' said Deanna. 'She sits there with a Walkman on, listening to them.'

'Maybe we should switch the tapes,' said Carol. 'A pair of tits would do wonders for her self-esteem. She's like a skeleton with hair. She probably reads the nutritional information on the sides of tissue boxes.'

'Why would they hunt her from Goldman's if she's that bad?' asked Deanna.

'People move about a lot in this business. And when did being good have anything to do with anything? They like to shuffle faces around every

31

now and then. It keeps people on their toes,' Carol said.

'I don't know anyone who's got a good word to say about her,' said Deanna, picking up the wine bottle and refilling everyone's glass, Carol's having emptied rather more swiftly than her own or Andrea's.

'Anderson might,' said Andrea. 'I heard that he was personally involved in recruiting her.'

Carol shook her head as she drew her glass away from her mouth and set it authoritatively down on the table. 'No. I know that for a fact. It was Martin alone who went out and got her. Surely he told you that?'

'That's not my style, Carol. I didn't talk about things like that with Martin. I didn't want to compromise either of us. I just have this feeling that she's here for a reason. Call it gut reaction, I don't know.' Andrea sighed.

'Knee-jerk reaction is more like it. Just relax. I haven't heard of anything unusual that's about to happen. Joannie just arrived,' Carol noted over Deanna's shoulder.

The manageress arrived with a handsome man probably half her age. The first thing Andrea noticed was her nails, painted flame red. Her hair had the casual elegance of something that had been worked on for hours. She was made up perfectly, pen and brush strokes going over her face as if it were a canvas, leaving a finished picture of sparkling sophistication.

'When I'm her age, I hope I look that good,' said Deanna.

'And have a boyfriend like that,' said Carol.

Andrea was still distracted by Gillian Kay. She did not want to appear paranoid or obsessed about her, least of all in front of Deanna and

Carol, but it gnawed at her. She buried the thought.

For the next two hours, they covered the usual range of topics. Who was sleeping with who, who was on the move, which accounts were up for grabs, rumours that had been heard, the latest Carl Anderson story – there was always at least one – and, one of the favourite topics of discussion, where they would go next in the industry. All of this continued in spite of their unwritten rule that they would not talk shop. All the conversations seemed to lead back there one way or another.

'So And, are you going to make a move on little Tim?' teased Deanna.

'I might,' she replied loftily.

'I think you should,' said Carol.

'Maybe I will,' said Andrea, not realising that the opportunity would present itself sooner than she realised.

Chapter Four

'WHAT'S WRONG WITH him?' she heard herself saying too anxiously into the phone. She was almost barking and tried to calm herself slightly. 'He's hurt himself. How?'

'He was carrying some of those boxes we're using for the archiving and he tripped over a loose trailing wire. He's just banged his head a bit, but he wants to see you.'

'Joan, can't you deal with it?'

Joan, the personnel officer, was the nearest DRA had to a health and safety officer, a first aider, a bomb warden. She was forever trying to organise jolly get-togethers. Joan was single. Joan did not answer her question.

'Oh all right,' she sighed as though she did not really want to go down there. 'Tell him I'll be down in a few minutes. Are you sure there's nothing too serious?'

'Do you mean like a possible claim against us? I wouldn't have thought so, but maybe that's why you should come down and see him, Andrea.'

After she put the phone down, she sat in her office for a minute or two, excited. For two days now she had been watching Tim Matthews methodically take files from the shelves outside the offices and put them in archive boxes. Other people in the office, his colleagues, were surprised that Tim had been asked to do the job, but his junior position in the planning department and his age seemed to cast him in the rôle of general dogsbody.

She thought about last night's conversation at Cranes, the way the girls had teased and badgered her about him. She thought about the prospect. Tim. Just nineteen and almost too pretty in that absurd way only home counties boys can be. About six feet tall with short light hair kept neat, he had started wearing his summer-weight suits that she remembered from last year, when he first arrived.

Two days of watching him bending over the files and humping boxes on to the trolley. Each day a different pair of trousers, each pair clinching his bum in a certain way and all she had to do was look up from her desk to see it through the window. She would be in the middle of conversations on the phone or even have people in the office with her and would have to look secretly over their shoulder as she saw him bend. She didn't want to miss a single chance to see his shirt fabric tighten over his back and his knees bend. And now he had tripped and hurt himself and was in the sick room on the ground floor wanting to see her. She inhaled.

As she rode in the back elevator alone, she looked at herself in the mirror that formed the back wall to it and adjusted her skirt slightly. She was feeling a little hot and all of a sudden her clothes didn't seem to fit any more, like they were trying to clamber off her body. The waistband of her skirt felt woolly on her stomach, her knickers like they were on the outside. Even so, she was looking good. 'Nice and easy, Andrea,' she said to herself as the indicator flashed a capital G and the doors shuddered back.

She swiped her card through the unit on the wall and opened the double doors. Joan was standing outside the door looking worried, which didn't bother Andrea because that was how she always looked. About thirty-seven, she was the matronly figure that a lot of the girls in the office would both take the mickey out of but quietly go to for advice on practical work things. She was the nearest thing they had to a union organiser in an otherwise aggressive environment.

'How is he, Joan, and what's all the drama for?'

'He has a small cut on his forehead. He only tripped rather than fell. No sign of concussion and I've treated . . .'

She decided to cut Joan off in the middle of her *Casualty* fantasy before she really got rolling. 'Okay Joan, but I think this is something you should have dealt with. I don't have any management line over Tim.'

'He insisted on seeing you. Maybe he's in shock.'

Andrea smiled at herself, amazed at Joan's ability to unknowingly place two sentences at a counterpoint that was amusing and insulting.

And Joan knew she was lying, Andrea could tell. She was too savvy not to know what had happened between her and Martin and that she had a not-so-secret yearning for young Tim Matthews, with his good school charm and smiling innocence. A yearning which Joan was standing in the way of at that moment.

'I'll handle it,' she said finally in a way Joan knew better than to argue with.

36

The sick room was on the ground floor just next door to the stationery storeroom. It was not used very often and she had only seen the inside of it twice before. She couldn't really remember how it looked or still less what it would be like adorned with Tim. She opened the green door slightly and almost slithered through the opening, as though she didn't want Joan to stand there and gawp through the gap.

There were two windows in the room which were both hung with blinds. They were the sort with hanging slats and one of them near the couch in the room was closed. The other was open slightly and the sun cut through it in sharp rays that seemed to burn the antiseptic medical smell of the room. It reminded her of the sick room at school where she would go for a lie down with tummy trouble or to get injected. The small sink in the corner, next to the glass cabinets containing tubes and bandages and scissors, had a funny limescale stain around the plughole that made it seem too old-fashioned for a modern building like DRA's. She felt as though she had stepped through the slit in the doorway and back in time.

Tim was leaning against the black leather couch, his behind rustling and crinkling against the body-length of tissue that was laid out on it. The couch was parallel with the window and the wall but kept slightly back from it to allow the heating system to work unobstructed. His green jacket was slung over one of the uncomfortably low armchairs and the top two buttons of his shirt were undone. She wasn't sure where his tie was. Letting her eyes travel from his shiny black brogues up to his crotch, which was suspended by the green wool of his suit trousers, she came to rest on his eyes and the small cut that sat next to the right one. It looked no more serious than a bad shaving cut.

'I hear someone's had a bit of a fall then,' she said, sounding even and detached.

'There were some wires from a printer. You know, on the second floor, near where we're stacking the boxes.'

'I thought you were using a trolley for the boxes. What made you carry them in the first place?'

'It was only the one box and it didn't seem worth it. Just a small one.' He smiled and she looked at his crotch again and then moved closer to him.

She put her hand up to his temple and touched his hairline, moving his head so the sun caught the cut full on.

'That doesn't seem too bad.'

He stayed leaning against the couch and the room was silent. She could feel his breath and almost hear his chest rising. Could he feel the same? She wanted to turn and face him and look him in the eyes more directly but instead she ran her hand only ever so slightly over the back of his head as she moved away and felt a tingle go up her arm as the hand crackled over the short hair.

'Are you going to be okay to carry on?' she said, looking more out of the window than at him.

'Well, Andrea, I did strain my groin a bit when I fell and I thought maybe you wanted to have a look at that while you were here.'

She looked at him and he was holding his bulge with one hand, the other still leaning casually on the couch. He was smiling and reminded her of one of those pop stars on television who shout and grab their balls all the time. His smirk seemed to indicate that she was meant to be in some way shocked or surprised by this. He obviously thought he had her where he wanted – embarrassed.

'Well I can't do it with your trousers on, can I, Tim?' she said, going over to the window and gently tugging the chain on the blind to cut the sun out of the room and leave them properly alone. Without looking at him, she went over to the door and clicked the street-door-type Yale lock so that it could only be opened from the inside. She took the phone off the hook. These were small and pointless precautions because no one came down there in any case but she enjoyed doing them as it gave a sense of ritual.

When she looked back at him, she was pleased to see the smirk had disappeared but disappointed that the trousers had not. Tim was standing now, nervously fingering his belt buckle and glancing at his crotch and then at her and then back again. He looked sheepish and like something had gone badly wrong. Andrea smiled to herself and looked at the poor lamb, out of his depth and feet hardly touching the bottom.

'Oh, didn't you hear me, Tim?' she whispered, her hands on his belt buckle, pulling the slack through the loops and hearing the sound the leather made against his waistband. She looked him directly in the eyes and zipped down his fly. He reached to touch the shoulders of her jacket, a favourite from the Paul Smith men's collection, and she told him not to. One, two, three, four, five. The buttons of his pale green shirt twisted in her fingers and then his shirt was open. His chest was almost hairless and his nipples small and pink but barely hairy.

She put her hands on his slim hips and felt the

bones under her palms. She ran her hands around his back, quickly running them up under his shoulder blades before bringing them to rest at the back of his trousers. She could feel boxer shorts protruding just over the top and ran her finger along them carefully as if they were a razor blade. She didn't want to hang about, so off came the shirt. He went to take off his watch but she told him not to.

This was to be the way of it. She had decided. There would be few questions and answers. He would respond to what she told him. He was where he should be. She had him at last and was not going to let him ask his way out of the situation. Her mind flashed back over the past few days and washed the memory over her excited thoughts and towards the coming few days. She saw it all in an instant and liked it.

Pulling him away from the couch, she undid the two buttons that were holding his trousers up. She dropped to her knees almost in time with the tumbling trousers and started to undo his shoe laces. She threw each black brogue on to the same armchair as his jacket and pulled his socks off like wrapping paper from a Christmas present. He didn't even have hair on the tops of his feet. As he lifted a foot at a time so she could take him out of his trousers, she started to wonder what his pubic hair would be like or even if he would have any. He was only in his boxer shorts now and she knew it wouldn't be long before she would find out.

Kneeling upright, she made a mental note to buy him some decent underwear, but at this juncture it was not so important what covered him as what he was. She put the heel of her hand on his crotch and felt the warmth of his cock, which was bent uncomfortably to the left. She opened the gap in the fly at the front and pushed on his balls. His cock sprang through the gap, making an entrance, and she saw he was fully erect.

The tip of his cock had a small covering of fluid that gathered near the eye at the top. She made a circular motion around it with her index finger and he whimpered slightly and opened his legs a few inches. She looked at the insides of his thigh and saw at last just a smattering of hair, but not hairy footballer's legs. Tim was a more likely candidate for the rowing eight. She pushed his knees silently together and looked up at him while she worked the boxers over his hips, past his knees and off his ankles.

Naked before her, it all seemed logical and perfect. This was where they were meant to be. She realised she wanted to kiss him and stood up and pulled him towards her. At first he looked unprepared but had obviously made his mind up by the time their lips met as he drew in a big breath just before they made contact.

And what contact. For a nineteen-year-old it was extraordinary, especially a naked and horny nineteen-year-old. She grabbed the cheeks of his backside and supported them, weighing each up in her hand. His cock was hard and seethed fluid which made her feel hotter and hotter as it lighted against the fabric of her skirt. She held his bum tighter and pulled him closer. As he reared away from her, the mark he left on her skirt was like spittle. She thought about how she would have to clean this off before they went back upstairs and it made her feel even sexier.

'Sit up on the couch,' she said, as she moved her hands down his behind and on to the backs of his legs, shoving them upwards in the direction she wanted him to go. As his rear made contact with the couch, she heard the tissue strain and tear under him. Feeling frantic, she ripped the tissue away from either side of him, exposing the smooth black leather of the couch, which was like a good purse. The only tissue remaining was that which his body weight had held on to. It formed a seat under him and where his legs were slightly apart she could see its whiteness between them and his balls resting on it. She put her hands on his knees and opened them wide enough to walk in between them. He was only slightly taller than her on this seat and she used his knees as a support to push herself up the few inches to make contact with his mouth once more.

He leaned forward, reaching his hands between his legs and the edge of the couch. He supported her hips, pulling her up to feed on his mouth which he had opened wide. As she explored over his back with her hands, counting the vertebrae, she could feel the skin on it tightening as he leaned further and further into her mouth. She was on tiptoe now and his hand massaged her, grinding skirt against knickers and knickers against fanny. The skirt was a little too long for him to hitch up and she was glad. She wanted him. She had waited this long and would survive a little longer.

In her mouth his cock swelled and pulsed. She had licked up and down the erection for what must have been agonizing moments for poor Tim. He shouted slightly and made some indecipherable shrieks in time with the jolts of his body. She tickled the sac of his balls with her index finger and he sighed and then looked at her in sudden surprise when she trailed her finger lower and separated his buttocks just slightly. But that would wait a few minutes.

She wanted him in her mouth again. She wanted to connect herself to him and hold him there. To bring him to the edge and then pull him back again. To make him yelp. He pushed his knees open and arched his back to get his cock deeper into her and she opened wider and dropped lower on to him as he did so. He held her head at the back and they stayed in position for a few moments, her eyes concentrating on his downy pubic hair and his eyes, she imagined, glazed over.

She started to work more concertedly on the head of his cock, smearing it with saliva and feeling it mix with the pre-come fluid of his own. Slowly at first, she made her mouth like a little tent covering his swollen head. The ridge of his phallus pulsed with blood and became a hard edge against her lips. She worked against this ridge, guessing that the tingle in her lips from the rub would be nothing compared to the one he was feeling. She kept on mouthing the tip and got faster in her movements. He had slowed his own thrusting and was content for her to set the speed. Faster still. His breathing became irregular and spare and she knew that unless she slowed down he would come and it was too soon for that. She kept the speed up for a moment longer and he gasped, throwing his hands back over the couch and on to the window-sill behind him. As he did so he knocked over some of the tubes and boxes that rested on it. She stopped moving her mouth over him and stood up quickly, while he was still thrown back.

He was breathing like someone who had been in a sprint race. She reached past him and picked up one of the tubes that lay on its side on the window-ledge. Reading the side of it quickly to check that it would be safe to use, she smiled at him as she screwed the cap off.

'Andrea . . .'

He might have been using her name as a question, a request or a statement, so she did not respond but simply lifted his ankles so that his feet were up on the couch and spread out to the side as far as they would go. His cock was erect and stood away from his body at an angle. His balls now barely touched the tissue under him, lifted as they were by the position of his legs and the force of his erection. She squeezed them in her hand. Then she squeezed the tube and some of the clear gel-like substance found her index finger. She put about as much as she would on a toothbrush. She looked at Tim and put her hand under his balls and reached lower down, to find what she was looking for.

He gasped with the coldness of the cream. She smeared it around the opening of his anus and got some on the cheeks where they protected it. She also took the opportunity to get some over her index and then middle finger, just in case. She kissed him quickly and then squeezed some cream on the tip of his cock, making him look like a Häagen-Dazs creation. She did not smear it over his cock, but just left it there and put some more on her index finger.

As she probed his anus he kept his eyes shut and gritted his teeth slightly, not showing any signs that he was not enjoying it. He was eager to please. She thought this would probably be a new experience for young Tim, nineteen and at his physical peak. Horsey seventeen-year-olds called Caroline probably didn't do this sort of thing. She made circular motions with her finger and his body moved in the same way. Her finger, so small and delicate, through a small opening in his body, was controlling his movements. She went in to her second knuckle on the middle of her finger, turning her hand slightly as she did so. He opened his eyes, wide. She slipped in all the way to her third knuckle, lifting her thumb so that it was under his balls.

Holding her finger there, she used her free hand to rub the cream over the head of his cock which was now pointing directly at the ceiling. When it was suitably smeared, she began to masturbate him slowly and then moved her finger inside him in time with her hand.

Whereas with one finger in him, his body had known which direction to move in, the combination of a finger deep inside him and a hand on his cock threw his body into turmoil. It was lost. He was lost. Pulled irresistibly in two directions of pleasure at the one time. The rhythm started slowly, in and out, up and down, the cream making a squelching sound. His breathing became heavy and sounded like he was only breathing in, not out. Like a balloon blowing itself up. Her pussy felt an itch that was crying out to be scratched and she moved her legs slightly as though she could rub the lips together to satisfy the urge.

The antiseptic room seemed very quiet all of a sudden. She was no longer at work. It was no longer day or night, here or there. The sun crept round the small gaps at the side of the blind and she remembered it was day-time.

Tim had begun to sweat and a sheen of it covered the little cut on his eye, her reason for being there. Slowly at first his body found a rhythm and gave in to it. His cock slipped around in her hand and she held it tightly to stop it getting away. He released a few little groans and she thought she heard her name somewhere in there. She worked her finger harder, curling it up and pushing it against the hidden gland at the back of his cock. She felt him tighten around the intrusive digit and he thrashed up off the couch, the single remaining scrap of tissue slipping from under him and falling to the floor. Sweat covered the couch where his rear had been and now he was lifting himself on his arms and his spread legs. He gulped once and looked directly at her.

His knees quivered as he ejaculated. It was like she had struck oil. She pushed his cock back at him so that the come covered his bare abdomen. Shining and almost clear, it looked like rain. He groaned and writhed as shot after shot seemed to force from him through the shine of the cream covering his cock, its eye opening slightly as he did so. He writhed away from her finger and she allowed it to slip through his now tight anus and plop out. She kept working on his cock with her hand, winding him up further and further while he clenched his eyes tightly shut and made an angry face, shaking his head as if he were saying no, or denying what was happening.

As he hung in oblivion in front of her, she desperately groped down to find the hem of her skirt and ripped it up like she was changing the blanket on a bed. Quickly getting her other hand down the front of her knickers, she worked deft fingers over her clitoris, leaning against the couch to steady herself. She looked at Tim's semen on his stomach and his cock still quivering and jumping every now and then.

She felt her orgasm coming quickly and easily

46

and was ready to let it take her where it wanted. There would be time later to take it easy. Her body tightened and she leaned against Tim as the first wave hit. She had hardly needed to touch herself. She gripped the couch and her foot brushed the piece of tissue on the ground. The second wave. She felt her breath pushing up her throat and escaping in the form of a small cry. She rode the wave and hung there in space, using Tim for support.

Their breathing took on the same pace and came down to normal together. She looked at Tim who smiled and said only 'Andrea,' and leant forward as though he were about to plant a kiss on her.

Avoiding his mouth, she bent down and picked up the tissue.

Chapter Five

AT EIGHT FORTY-five on Thursday morning, the air in the hotel conference room hung heavy with expectation and hangovers. A haze of alcohol seemed to linger in the room, most attendees for MCC2 having arrived the night before and proceeded straight to the bar.

They were on the top floor of the hotel, a penthouse conference room, almost, and the sun was shining brightly through the double-aspect windows. Too brightly for some people, it seemed, as they groaned and whimpered. Andrea saw the familiar post-expenses-drinking-binge look in many eyes. She had not travelled down until later and had avoided the bar.

The dress code today was casual. They had been instructed specifically to be jeans-casual. Presumably any divergence from this path would be viewed with suspicion and interest by the cod psychologists who coordinated the course. Andrea wore a faded pair of Gap jeans and a blouse from Principles. Her only nod upmarket was a loose-knit Calvin Klein sweater in oatmeal. On her feet she wore clumpy Doctor Marten's and fluffy white socks. She enjoyed the feel of the jeans against her rear, her underwear sheer across her backside.

It was a standard set-up for a small meeting room being used for a training course. Overhead projector, a couple of flip charts and two video cameras. The video recorder was wired in to two large television screens at the front of the room. Tables were arranged in three sides of a square. Coffee had been on the go since eight-thirty, but not much else had.

At the front of the room, Martin Cox and David Wheeler were conferring in whispers. They were the two DRA managers selected to oversee the course. Independent third party trainers were also present from the company that had designed the course, which had been tailored to the specific needs of DRA.

The door to the room opened and Carl Anderson, head of the agency, walked in. As he did, Andrea felt every back in the room straighten slightly.

Carl Anderson never dressed casually. The first thing you always noticed about him was his clothes. He wore an expensive dark double-breasted suit. On other people it would have looked like a jaded attempt at power dressing but on Carl it looked perfectly natural. He was powerful and he dressed that way. Now in his mid-forties, his hair had receded an inch or so and he swept it back over his head in a thick dark mane that was streaked with silver. Again, on anyone else, it would have looked like a mid-eighties advertising cliché, but on Carl Anderson it fitted. Carl was able to move beyond a stereotype or straight cliché and breathe life into it. His mouth was a thin straight line running a perfect horizontal under his stout nose. His pupils seemed to fill most of his small eyes and his face was jowly, a mixture of business lunches and rigorous sessions on the Lifecycle. Nobody liked to wonder if Anderson had a sex-life.

Amongst the group, a wave of controlled fear took hold. Any small trace of guilt, a minor misdemeanour, an overclaim on expenses, a phone call not returned to a client, were amplified in each individual consciousness until they felt like signs around their necks. If Carl Anderson had stood there silently for long enough, Andrea was sure people would have stood up and started confessing to things, whether they had done them or not. He would have made an excellent police interrogator – or a murderer.

Carl Anderson scanned the expectant, fearful faces. He looked out of the window and the sun caught his profile. He began.

'The Chinese curse "May you live in interesting times" means nothing to us. In my times in this industry, there has never been a time that was not interesting. Never a dull moment, you could say. Constantly, we are changing. Our clients change. New products come to market, requiring new and different campaigns. Even when we go back and steal from the past, we do it to be different. To change. People change.'

He paused.

'Paul Deakin was fond of saying, simply and with a shrug, "Things change". DRA must change. We are about to enter a new time. We must live in new times. The new period will be most strenuous, for all of us. Let me say now, if anyone, anyone, does not feel they wish to be a part of the new times, of the change, they should leave. Now. Things will change.'

There was silence in the room. The sun felt

hotter than it had only a few moments earlier.

'The creative direction of this agency is floundering. I look around and I see good work. Average work. Simply bad work. I see a loose amalgam but what I do not see is any synergy, synchronicity – pick your own eighties word. The truth is that the words may have changed but the underlying reality has not. Things must change.

'I am sure that none of us would like to think of ourselves as traditionalists. Do any of us consider ourselves revolutionaries? Renaissance people? Many aspects of these issues will be covered by your purpose for being here today, this course. Many of you may be wondering why I am here. You are probably thinking that I am rambling, by now. Let me draw the threads together.

'Change.' He stopped for several seconds, letting the word flow over them.

'Within the next month, there will be a new appointment at DRA. A Director of Creative Affairs. For DRA, a departure. For me, a departure. I have decided that such an appointment will be, should be, in-house. Let me be unequivocal about this. There are no obvious candidates for this position in any sense of the word obvious.'

Andrea assimilated the speech. Anderson had always set the pace, called the tune. He would never let control slip from his grasp. Every other agency their size had some sort of Creative Director. Not DRA. It had grown from a three-man operation, but certain things had never changed. She wondered what Anderson was up to. Either DRA was about to buy another agency or be bought by one. Either way, Mike Mitchell, Deanna's boss, must be on his way out. Had probably already been fired by Anderson that morning. He wasted no time.

'You are privileged,' he continued. 'The first people to hear of this. All the other principals will be informed shortly. Beyond these, I want it to go no further. I will be meeting with Martin and David along with Carol.' No mention of Mike Mitchell, the whole room already mourning his passing. He gestured towards himself. 'Watch this space.'

He was gone.

The first people Andrea looked towards were Martin Cox and David Wheeler. They had not expected it either. Anderson was gaming as usual. They must have known he would be attending, which was why they were so engrossed in each other before Anderson arrived. They were wondering what he wanted. It would not have been beyond him to fire someone at that sort of meeting. The thing that got to everyone at DRA, that really found its way under their skins, was that despite all his antics, Carl Anderson was an impressive agency head and one who commanded their respect.

The next person Andrea looked at, instinctively, was Gillian Kay. Gillian was looking smug and self-satisfied, probably already choosing the furniture for her new office. Surely Anderson didn't bring her in six months ago just to promote her now? There would be no point in that. No connection between the events, despite what Gillian might want other people or even herself to believe. Andrea quickly appraised Gillian's casual clothes and stored a comment she would be able to make later about gardening.

'Well,' Martin was saying in his best I'm-in-control-honestly voice, 'after that intro I think the video needs little build-up from me.'

*

After the communal lunch, Andrea went off to her room to make a few calls. She wanted to speak to Deanna to see if she would be able to pump Carol for any information. She doubted that Anderson had genuinely not spoken to anyone about the new position prior to that meeting. She expected that everyone would want to fight their own corner, but she hoped she could rely on Deanna and Carol.

'Hi Deanna, it's Andrea. How are you?'

'Without a boss,' she said.

'I thought as much. Anderson came here this morning and made an announcement that he's going to appoint a Director of Creative Affairs at DRA.'

'Mike called me this morning. He said he wouldn't be coming into the office until later on this evening to collect his stuff,' said Deanna. 'What do you think he'll do?' She sounded upset.

'He'll be fine. He's well liked in the industry. He'll probably have his own agency in six months. Can you have a chat with Carol and see if she knows anything about this director position?'

There was a knock on the door. She checked her watch. It was still another twenty minutes before they were due back.

'Deanna, there's someone at the door. I'll call you later, okay? Who is it?' she called out.

'Room service,' came a muffled voice.

'Sorry?' she said, a questioning frown on her face as she opened the door.

It was Mike, the barman.

'Aren't you supposed to be carrying a tray or something?' she said to him sarcastically.

'It depends on what you've ordered,' he replied.

'And next you're going to tell me this is on the

menu, right?' she said, reaching out and squeezing his cock which was showing prominently through his uniform trousers.

He was uncertain of himself. Not sure what to say, she could tell. So was she, but for different reasons. It was not long before she had to be back on the course. She made a few quick decisions in her head.

'What do you think you can deliver in fifteen minutes?' she asked, pulling him into the room.

They fell to the floor in the small hall of the hotel room. He was on top of her immediately, hands fiddling and exploring the front of her jeans. With both hands he gripped the waistband and pulled. The buttons on the flies popped one by one, the sound of brass through the small fabric eyes. Their breathing was hot. He pulled her jeans to her ankles and left them there, bunched up on her DMs.

Little time was wasted on her underwear, despite its sexy white lacy cut, high on her legs and close into her crotch. Mike shoved them down, Andrea lifting her rear, and he bundled them up at her ankles as well.

Andrea lay on the carpet of the hotel floor, feeling its roughness against her legs and backside. Her clothes felt heavy around her ankles, her legs naked and her pussy bared. She found being naked from the waist down a sexy experience. It was as if her aching clit was the most prominent part of her. It was lunchtime, for Christ's sake. Why did she do it? Sometimes she wondered. When Mike gently fingered her pussy, she remembered the reason why.

'Mike, hurry up and fuck me,' she moaned.

He quickly undid his trousers and pushed them down to his knees, taking his boxer shorts with them at the same time. He was inside of her immediately. He had grabbed his strained cock and simply pushed it inside her. She was already wet and gasping to be filled, so it was a welcome intrusion.

As though he had realised time was of the essence, he fucked her fast and hard. He shoved into her, her pussy tight from the position of her legs, which were bound together at the ankles by her jeans. There was a friction of his pubic hair against hers, his cock opening her and her lips drawing him in.

Her buttocks were ground into the carpet by his plunges into her. She leaned her head against the floor and there as well the carpet rubbed against her. The top half of her body, still clothed, started to feel feverish, sweat building up under her blouse. Wettest of all, her pussy, in a way all its own. He pumped her, back and forth, in and out. His cock reaching into her, filling her and readying her.

'Uh . . . oh,' Mike was moaning against her ear.

She grabbed his buttocks and pulled him into her and herself towards him as she had her orgasm. Lifting her shoulders off the floor as she ran her hands up his back and latched on to his shirt-clad shoulders. She drove her body hard into his, smelling the sweet perspiration of sex their bodies had created. She shoved her head against his shoulder and hammered herself against his tight body, crying out and shouting through the haze of sex and sweat.

She clung to him in desperate agony as she felt his orgasm. She contracted the walls of her vagina around him, her orgasm rippling on in time with her muscles. He gripped her tightly to him and she felt a pulse and then his come spurt inside her, the movements of his cock tight and hard.

She arrived ten minutes late for the start of the afternoon session. A video was in progress and Andrea walked to her seat, wetness still seeping into her knickers.

'Sorry. Something came up,' she smiled to Martin.

Chapter Six

'WELL, *THIS IS* a surprise,' she said, leaving him at the door and not making any movement to suggest she wanted him to enter. Not right now anyway.

'But is it a nice surprise, Andrea?'

'Let's just say it is a little unexpected. I assume you didn't happen to be just passing?'

He smiled with a mixture of self-assurance and arrogance and although she hated herself for it, she began to soften. She had let her white towelling robe open ever so slightly at the front and she could feel a gentle breeze on her cleavage, as though a window was open somewhere along the plush hotel corridor. She thought of her last encounter in the hotel room – the one with Mike, the barman, earlier that afternoon.

She was in the sort of mood where she did not really know what she wanted to do. Like a really boring Sunday afternoon with her parents. She felt like a piece of rag that had slowly had all the water squeezed from it.

Tim's appearance at the door had opened up new possibilities. She shifted her bare feet slightly on the deep grey carpet beneath them and saw Tim glance down at them, taking in every possible inch of nudity that she had to offer. She realised she was ready to offer more.

It had been an exhausting day, spent mostly in the aftershock of Carl Anderson's appearance. Perhaps she would tell Tim about it, at some point, but she was at the end of a draining day and wanted him to hold her. And to fuck her. To make love to her gently and then hard. She wanted to feel his body move against hers, generating heat. She wanted to run her hands over his naked young body, keeping every bit of it for herself, making him hers. She wanted to give herself to him, to let him have her and do what he wanted to, and with, her. A surge went through her as all these thoughts and feelings seemed to funnel through her and end down between her legs – where she wanted him.

He looked very blue in terms of his clothing. His jeans were sky blue with button flies that seemed to hug around his crotch and had a well worn and used look. It was as though a boxing glove were hanging off his belt, the way his crotch just stood there. His shirt was the same material and almost the same colour as his jeans. The black leather part of the ensemble was a thick belt and his black shoes. The dim overhead light in the hotel-room doorway caught the silver on the oversized buckle of his belt and her eyes held on it for a moment before sliding lower and back to the buttons on his flies which she could hear calling out to her. He held a white plastic bag that seemed to have most of its contents in the bottom as it swung low and heavy.

'Is that your toothbrush?'

'I've bought you a present.'

'Oh. That's thoughtful of you, Tim. When do I get to see it?'

'You have to let me in first,' he said, grinning.

Well, she thought, they couldn't stand there all night like a coffee advert, so she moved away to let him through the door and felt the lightest of draughts as he moved past her. She caught a nose of the aftershave she had bought him. His skin was set off perfectly against the blue of his shirt and she remembered how he looked naked. She brushed one hand against his rear as he passed her.

Andrea closed the door and caught up with him. As he placed his carrier bag on the bed, she spun him around by his shoulder and kissed him. He opened his mouth wide and she felt herself lost in his kiss, making her lips purse slightly so she could enter his mouth and go to the very centre of him. Her hands glided over the denim of his shirt and the cotton felt smooth. The rear pockets of his jeans protruded and she let her thumbs hang in them as they both began to move.

Tim had begun to push open the towelling dressing gown and now only the belt was wrapped all the way around her, both sides of the gown open and bunched up under it. She grasped quickly and undid the flimsy knot that was holding her in check. As it released, so did she. The robe dropped to the floor and she was nude before him. She wanted to rub her whole body, every inch of her, against the blue vision in front of her. To release the pressure that was inside of her. She lay her head on his chest as they stood near the end of the bed.

'Tim, make love to me. Please.'

He ran his hand through her hair, which was still slightly damp from the shower. The hair between her legs was also damp, and becoming more so. He looked at her with steel-blue eyes and she was awash with the colour, could feel it rinsing her through and making her fresh everywhere. She wanted him to take her. She moved back from him and lay face down on the bed, waiting.

Focusing on the phone by the side of the bed, she heard him undo his belt buckle. It made a small metallic clank as it brushed against something, probably the buttons on his fly. She looked over her shoulder and saw him undo just the top button and then pull the top of his jeans so the rest of them burst open. She caught a glimpse of his erection under his shirt just before she turned her head back and looked only at the bedclothes.

The shirt came off. He kicked off his shoes and then she heard him hop from foot to foot as he took off his socks. The jeans sounded heavy as they hit the floor. A few seconds later, his underwear did not sound as weighty. She closed her eyes, thinking only of the weight held in by the underwear.

The mattress sagged and she felt him get on the bed. He held her ankles and opened her legs. Kneeling between them with his hands either side of her shoulders, he dipped down and kissed her on the back of the neck. She felt his cock brush gently on her buttocks. It was warm and firm. He gyrated his hips and rubbed his cock slowly over her rear. He let out a breath that was hot on the side of her face. She squirmed harder against the bed, trying to find an edge to move with.

He reached down between her legs and she opened them wider as he caressed and tickled her lips. He ran a thumb up the crevice of her backside and then his whole hand came back down in one swift movement as he slid his middle finger deep into her pussy. She was shocked by the speed and smoothness of the entry and inched herself up the bed as if to get away from him. He moved his hand with her.

They were still for a moment. She raised herself up on her knees and again his hand followed her movements. Again they were still. He was going to make her do the work, if that was what she wanted. She did.

She rocked slowly at first using her knees and hands as easy pivots. Backwards and forwards she went on to his finger, feeling also the pressure of his thumb on the inside of her thigh where he used it as a lever. Occasionally he would move his finger slightly to gain some depth, and she could feel it against the sensitive pad behind her clit. She stopped.

'More, Tim.'

Another finger. She sighed.

'Please.'

A third finger. She gasped. As she did so, he began working his hand against her and this time she moved very quickly up the bed, but he was right behind her. She buried her face in the pillow and arched her back. She felt wide open and full up all at once. His fingers were slightly rough and did not feel part of her in the way his cock did when it was inside her. The flat of his hand rested against her bottom and it felt like he was cupping all of her in his hand. She could feel his three fingers crossing over each other every now and then.

The rhythm was low and intense, making her lower body throb and then gush upwards. She could feel her thighs beginning to sweat where Tim's hands were touching them. The thumping inside her was communicating itself rapidly to her clitoris which was responding in kind. This would not take long, she thought. She reached up and held the headboard as she started to feel herself coming. She whimpered and called his name and he put his free hand on the back of her neck, holding her steady as she climaxed in heated bursts. With a sudden pop, she was empty and breathless. He rested his hand on her rear.

She rolled on to her side to see him kneeling there, his cock stiff and pointing off to one side. She reached for it and he surprised her by moving back.

'Not yet,' he said. 'I want you to have a bit more first.'

He disappeared over the edge of the bed, and she heard the crinkle of the white plastic bag.

There were two dildos. Both had the brown fleshy colour she had become familiar with over the years. One was quite long, about nine inches, although quite slim. The other was a double vibrator. The main dick on this was nice and broad-looking and probably six or seven inches. The smaller finger-like part looked snakishly slim and able to penetrate. Tim had obviously been doing a little homework.

'This one first,' she said, lifting the single long dildo from his hand and twisting the base. It came to life in her hands and felt like a weapon. Inside, she felt herself hum in time with the pulsating cock and she ran moist.

She sat up slightly against the headboard and opened her knees wide. She played the tip around her hole but only just enough to lubricate it with a film of her passion. She jumped back from it when it touched her quivering clitoris as though a small electrical charge were running through it. Tim was watching intently, like a boy making a model aeroplane. She noticed that his cock seemed even stiffer than it had only moments earlier. She would have liked to have that in her as well, but right at that moment she wanted him to inflict the dildos, both of them, on her. Before handing it back to him, she let the tip vibrate against her tongue and tasted herself on it.

He was rough where she had been smooth. He simply shoved the plastic cock into her for the first few inches and then held a firm pressure on it until it was in almost to the hilt. She was worried he was going to lose it in her. His face was gleeful. She dropped her knees back slightly. He began to make very short jerking movements to stab the dildo in and out of her, moving it only an inch or so to and from her vagina. She began to pulse her buttocks in time with him and ease herself forward in time with the miniature thrusts.

She reached towards her knees and stroked his right arm, watching the muscles flex in it as he moved continuously back and forth. Her own muscles began to tremble around the invasion in her pussy. She closed her eyes and in her imagination the dildo and she were the same size, almost indistinguishable from each other. In the darkness of her eyes a yellow began to appear. It was like an out of body experience and she watched herself from above, writhing against the dildo. She opened her eyes and they were blurred, Tim somewhere up there through the misty waters, gritting his teeth and staring intently. She cried out and held his arm as she came. He kept the cock moving inside her and in doing so jerked her arm up and down with his own.

But he did not stop. He began pulling out the vibrator just a little further. She could mostly tell this by the way the buzzing became slightly louder – her pussy was tingling too much to make an accurate assessment of what was happening to her down there. He carried on with the longer thrusts, her lips alive and clitoris firm. She came down from her second orgasm and orbited in a dazed and relaxed way. Tim was still fully erect and she marvelled at his self-control. Very carefully he removed the vibrator from her, leaving her feeling ravaged and empty, as though she had been robbed.

She knew what he would want to do next.

Without speaking, he produced the double dildo and a thrill went through her at the prospect of another part of her joining in the proceedings.

'Do you have something to grease that with?' she asked him.

From his carrier bag of tricks came a small jar. He removed the lid and was about to dip his fingers in when she took it from him. She dipped in, gathered a dollop and then found the small cleft between her buttocks. The cream was cold and her finger sharp. Soon she was loose and pliable. She turned on her side and drew her knees up to her chest, displaying two entrances at once.

The longer of the two cocks on the dual dildo parted her lips and entered her first. Its buzz stimulated her around the entrance of her vagina and promised deeper pleasures to come. As it advanced, she felt the tip of the smaller secondary shaft rest on her anus. She pulled her knees up tightly to her chest, opening herself fully.

As it entered her rear, the plastic cock felt exactly the right size. It was not so big that it stretched her painfully but nor was it so small and thin that it was unnoticeable. It opened her and shaped her anus around itself to just the right degree, as though it was made for her and was meant to be there. The sensation it gave caused her to forget momentarily that a corresponding but larger cock was making a similar journey into her pussy. She was being explored in two areas at once, the one feeding the other and back again. She was not sure how long she would be able to hold out against such contending pleasures.

She lay on her side, both cocks now fully inside of her, thanks to Tim. He knelt on the bed and fed them into her like a technician. Now he slowed the vibrator down, the buzz going from a fast high-pitched feeling to a much lower and more rumbling oscillation.

This time, instead of driving in and out of her, Tim made a circular motion with the base of the dildo. The effect was amplified by the time it reached the tips of the cocks that impaled her. It made her looser around them and the force of Tim's motion caused her to sink deeper into the mattress. It was a powerful and intense action, not quite painful but definitely pleasurable. She wanted it to continue, the feeling of being plumbed and mined by these fake cocks. She wanted them to touch her in places a real cock never could, to bring her to a more intense climax than a cock alone ever could.

Her toes rubbed the cover of the bed. Tim rested his free hand on her hip-bone which was protruding through her soft flesh due to the position of her body. She could only just see him from the position she was lying in. This was the boy at the office. The one who moved files around, did research for her. The one who would go around and talk and smile with everyone, flirting with all the girls. And now, here he was in a hotel room with her, naked and working a double dildo in and out of her, with an enormous erection of his own that looked fit to burst at any moment.

She remembered Tim in the sick room, his spunk bursting from his cock and the look of tight passion on his face as it did. She thought of the way he had looked when he entered the room earlier, dressed all in light blue with his muscular body brushed by it and the tightness of his jeans, front and back. The sounds of him undressing, making his body naked. The way he had brought her off, first with fingers, then with a dildo and now with this.

All of these thoughts and feelings combined suddenly and it all made sense to her. She no longer needed words or even images to describe her feelings. The only things she had to explain the intense feelings were feelings even more intense. It was not something worth putting into language. To do so would have been to change it and tarnish it forever. It would have been an attempt to keep and preserve the passion instead of going with her feelings as and when they happened.

Just before she came, for perhaps less than a second, she felt both orifices relax and open as though they had given up. For just a split second, in the blink of an eyelid, she had revealed herself in her entirety and was completely vulnerable. Then she closed up and tensed, ready for the physical uproar that was about to happen.

She orgasmed around the invasions and

treasured the moment, the feeling of pleasure, of intimacy and of knowledge of herself. Tim was there, somewhere, balled up in the feelings and the passion, the shouts and the cries, the movements against the sheet. She pounded the bed with the side of her fist, calling out as the third orgasm took her. Against her rear she felt a warm spatter and knew that Tim had been unable to wait any longer.

He bucked and rocked on the bed, pushing his hips and running his hands over himself, the dildo forgotten. His spunk flew and arced through the air, some of it finishing on the mattress and some on her.

The dildo still inside of her, she felt herself drift into a doze as Tim rested his weight on her.

Chapter Seven

ANDREA TOOK THE proffered dish and let her hand brush then linger over Jerome's, catching Tim's angry scowl from across the other side of the table.

'Thanks, Jerome,' she said, injecting a trace of huskiness into her voice as though she'd just risen from a wild night.

'You're welcome, darling. Any time.'

'Any time?' she repeated with an exaggerated question mark, one eye on Tim the whole time.

Jerome just giggled.

On the way to the dinner party, she had needled Tim about Jerome. That he would be there and how gorgeous he was. She was testing Tim's jealous streak, to see if he had one. Apparently he did. She knew that he had not really wanted to go. Partly because he did not feel comfortable with the idea of meeting some of her acquaintances and mostly because he wanted to spend all evening with her, fucking her senseless before she left for Rome in the morning. He had not been pleased when she told him she would rather he didn't stay over because her flight was early. That, plus a few nicely timed flirtatious remarks from her to Jerome, and back again, meant that an angry desire would be simmering away in Tim. She wanted it to boil a while longer before she let it spill over.

The small group around the table consisted of people she knew relatively well. Well enough to feel comfortable and happy in their company. The criss-cross of friendships and acquaintances, friends of friends, was such that she found it difficult to remember quite who knew who and how. She was pleased at the admiring glances the women had given Tim. Anna and Claire, there with boyfriend and husband respectively, had exchanged knowing glances when she introduced them to him. Paula, perennially single and hence there on her own, had simply gawped.

She sipped from her wine, her third glass, and felt herself relax. Deanna, hostess that she was, must have spent ages peeling kiwi fruits and these were being passed round. Andrea took a bite into the succulent green flesh and let the juice mix with the taste of the wine. The kiwi was slightly acid on her tongue, a dribble of juice ran from the corner of her mouth and she smoothed it away with a finger. Dinner had been fish, chargrilled and seasoned with herbs that lingered on her palette.

Jerome was saying something loudly, people around the table laughing along. Andrea felt as though she were observing it from a distance, the wave of calm and relaxation soothing over her. The music was subdued and the candles played shadows across the white linen table-cloth.

Tim was looking at her. Had been looking at her most of the evening since they sat down to dinner. She could see he was annoyed with her, his jaw set firmly and his eyes just a fraction more

69

downcast than usual. She took pity on him, knowing it was unfair to get a rise out of him in this way, but she hoped it would be worth it. Part of her felt like she was manipulating him but the other was ready to be told off by him for being a naughty girl. A jolt of excitement went off between her legs.

'Is Tim going to Rome with you?' Jerome was asking.

'No, just me. We can't justify more than one person on a field trip,' she answered.

'Oh please, a field trip,' Jerome said rolling his eyes. 'You jet off to some European country and go shopping, and you call it a field trip. Still, I'm sure you'll find plenty to amuse you while you're there. I remember the stories from last time.'

Andrea thought she saw Tim sit bolt upright, as though he was about to leap from his chair and shout at Jerome – or her. She saw the rage boiling in him and hoped the anger would be reflected in his cock and that he would take it out on her and in her. It was as if she were having her foreplay with Jerome in preparation for sex with Tim.

'Will you excuse me for a moment, Jerome,' she said, rising gently and brushing his hand which was resting towards her on the table-cloth. She dropped her napkin onto the table and left the room.

She was barely halfway up the stairs when she heard footsteps behind her.

'Andrea, what the fuck's going on?'

It was Tim.

'Well,' she said, continuing her assent, 'I'm going to the bathroom.'

'Don't, Andrea.'

'What? Go to the bathroom?'

'You know what I mean,' he said.

She stopped on the stairs and turned to look down on him, two steps away from her. The light from the landing shone down on his face and she wanted him. It was that simple. He was wearing a polo shirt and the soft blue trousers from a casual two-piece suit. She wanted to reach out and touch his hair, run her hand along the side of his head. She held herself in check.

'Tim, don't be stupid, okay?'

'You've been flirting with Jerome all fucking night.'

She exhaled and carried on up the stairs towards the bathroom, Tim in tow. She turned when she reached the door.

'You're not going to follow me in here, are you?'

'I want to talk to you. We need to talk.'

'Tim, I've known Jerome for years, okay? Do you think I fancy him? Is that it?' She paused. 'So what if I do?'

She pulled the cord and went into the bathroom. Tim dodged in and closed the door behind him. They faced each other. She wanted to look down at his crotch to see if he was hard, but she could sense he was. He had the edge in his voice. She wondered if she should say anything else or if that would push him over the edge and make him storm off. She looked at him and then cast her eyes down, looking contrite.

He grabbed her by the hips and pulled her to him. She felt his body hard against her own. He kissed her, his head slightly to one side, his tongue working deep inside of her mouth almost immediately. She touched his shoulders only lightly, not wanting to disturb him in flow. Against her groin she felt his cock pushing at her, nudging her and awakening her down there.

Roughly, he pushed her away, shoving her back against the door, his face a mixture of anger and confusion. Already she could hear his breath, irregular and panting with excitement. Her pussy was moist and she wanted him in her, wanted him to take it out on her. She stayed still as his hands ran up the sides of her short skirt and grabbed at her knickers. They were down round her thighs in seconds.

She gasped as he fingered her. Like a piston his digit worked on her, so different and alien to her own, his finger long and seeming to go deep into her, spreading her lips and disappearing into her depths. With his thumb he made rotations around her clit, pushing it from side to side as it swelled. She moved her legs together when he pulled her panties off and he made her open them again, pushing her feet wider apart with one of his own.

Fully clothed with the exception of her underwear, she was even more conscious of her pussy than if she'd been naked. It was the only sexy place Tim could have access to at that moment and if he wanted to give her pleasure and have some of his own, that was where he would have to focus. And he was.

Now with two fingers inside her and his thumb still rubbing her clit, Tim was moving his whole arm. She wondered if the people downstairs would hear them or if they knew what they were up to. She didn't care. She wanted Tim to fuck her then she'd go down and have coffee with his come still inside her. On the way home, when he was happy again, she'd tell him the truth about Jerome – he was gay. But all that was for later. She turned her concentration to herself and to Tim's hand roving between her legs.

Andrea pumped her groin out in time with Tim's inward plunge but he pushed her hips back against the wall by using the palm of his hand against her pubic hair. The wall against her rear made her pussy feel like it was pushed into a small space, a tiny claustrophobic area that Tim was invading. She hoped that he would fuck her soon, but she did not dare interrupt his flow.

His hand left her and she tingled in its absence, wanting something deeper and harder in there. Something bigger. Tim's fingers had roused her pussy from its relaxed slumber. The gentle dinner-table consideration of whether or not to make love with Tim had been overtaken by the harsh reality of sex. She watched as he unzipped his fly. She wanted to grab his buttocks as he fucked her, to feel them moving back and forth, tensing and un-tensing as he drove into her. She hoped he would take his trousers down. As if he was reading her mind, he undid the button that held them together and pushed them down in a single movement at the same time as his boxer shorts.

She gasped when she saw him. His cock was flame-red on the tip and a raging mauve on the glans. It looked as though it were burning deep with his desire for her, mixed with his anger. She was not yet as wet as she would have liked, but the very sight of him aroused made her brim.

Tim massaged himself several times, outlining his hardness and size. He squeezed himself at the base of his cock and Andrea saw the blood fill him in a deep pulse that echoed on profoundly in her. Fluid seeped from the top of Tim's cock and he pointed it towards her, his eyes fixed on it. She had not remembered him so large. Perhaps she had shrunk back from him and he now seemed out of proportion.

Still pointing his cock at her, Tim advanced slowly towards her. The whole scene was playing out in slow motion and Andrea waited desperate moments until the initial contact from the scalding red point of Tim's cock. Her tight short skirt was hoisted up around her waist, bunched up and self-supporting.

With no ceremony or care, she felt herself entered. He immediately slipped his cock in deeply and fully, their pubic hairs touching and juice from her pussy running on to the base of his cock. Her legs were awkwardly apart and the standing position put her pussy at an angle that was deliciously out of step with Tim's member. Tim gave out a grunt, as though he had made his point, and rested his head against the bathroom door. She reached down and felt his rear, firm and taut under her fingers as she feathered over it with them.

On tiptoe, with Tim crouching and his knees bent, she ground herself onto him several times, grabbing his head as she did so. The contrasting angles of their bodies, contorted to accommodate each other, was pleasurable in a slow and sensuous way, but it was not what Andrea wanted at that moment.

She put her arms around Tim's shoulders and held on tight. Relaxing her legs so that her knees were slightly bent, she shuddered as Tim's hands held her at the back of her thighs. As he swept her legs up, she used her arms on his shoulders to climb him, careful to keep his cock inside of her although she doubted it would have slipped out in its current state. With her legs around his waist and her thighs gripping his hips, she hung on to him. He supported the weight of her slender body with ease.

Tim's hands gripped her rear and he moved her away from the bathroom door, taking half steps so as not to be tripped up by his trousers. They stood in the middle of the small room, the overhead light burning brightly.

Using her legs for leverage, Andrea moved up and down Tim's cock, conscious of the slide of their bodies, their juices a lubricant between the two of them, oiling them and making them work in a common motion. He was far inside her and their position only allowed the smallest arc of movement, the thrusts restricted, pleasuring the walls of her vagina. The soft wool of Tim's polo shirt shifted and crackled against the sleeves of her blouse. Tim bucked his hips as he held her, the anger still evident from the way he jabbed at her.

He moved with her again, pinning her against a wall, which she relaxed her back against. It supported her weight and freed Tim to take control. Squeezing him with her legs and then relaxing, she let him take over.

He fucked her hard and fast. His hands cupped her buttocks, pulling her wider open and his solid cock moved against the soft wetness of her. The top of his shaft grazed along her slit sending shock waves through to her clitoris, engorged and sensitive. It was an invasion and a retreat combined as he entered her, left her and re-entered her. She felt like clockwork, as though each lunge was winding her further and further up, her senses becoming taut like a coiled spring.

She closed her eyes tightly and grimaced, her mouth baring teeth. She whimpered and let out the occasional sniffle to help Tim along the way. She couldn't imagine what was really going on in his mind. The only palpable evidence she had was what he was doing to her now – ramming his cock into her with a force she hadn't expected him to have. She rested her head on his shoulder and opened her eyes, seeing the side of his neck, the soft skin and the hair on the back of it catching the light.

The tiles on the wall, which had been cold at the first touch, now warmed under her rear and became sweaty. She could feel the ridges where the tiles bordered each other and as Tim pushed against her, the ridges stimulated her. Her skirt remained bunched up around her waist, Tim's hands preventing it from sliding down.

'Oh Tim, that's it. Fuck me, go on.'

At her words he made a sneering sound and burrowed into her, overcoming her totally and filling her senses. She had been shaken roughly from her earlier relaxed state. This was the price to be paid, she thought. And it was not an unpleasant price. She hung on to Tim, sandwiched between him and the wall, and let the attack assail her faculties. He was in her in every sense. She felt him deep in her pussy and against her clit. She heard him breathing and grunting at her and she looked at him, straining her eyes to see his wool-clad back moving and rolling with exertion.

'Kiss me,' she said, wanting to taste him.

His mouth lingered on her, smothering her and stealing breath away from her. She inhaled through her nose to keep from drowning in him. His mouth was warm and soft, a contrast to the continuous dense thrust that was routing itself between her legs. His lips were pliable and the tip of his tongue came through them, lighting on her own. She buried her face into his, connecting to him, their breath passing from one to the other.

The fucking had been so intense that she had no way to judge how close Tim was to coming. None of the foreplay niceties of slow gentle love-making had taken place. The whole time he had been fucking her, the speed and rhythm was of someone about to come. She sensed an orgasm of her own, not far off. She wondered if she could come without him knowing, keep it to herself, for herself. He would surely feel her contract around him, but she could keep it quiet until that point. Spring it on him when he least expected it.

For the next minute or so, Andrea gritted her teeth and let herself be banged against the wall by Tim, still pissed off at her and still infatuated with her – a delicious combination. He drove into her in an exacting fashion. Her body became more rigid as her orgasm neared. She held her spine straighter and clung to Tim for dear life. She wanted to cry out, but did not, for fear of giving herself away. A flutter, somewhere between her chest and groin.

The clockwork feeling came back again. She was wound fully, her body tense and rigid, sexual energy about to release itself from her. The orgasm came like a breeze, blowing around the harsh edges of her body, cushioning her and comforting her, giving her the liberation she desired. She held onto the intensity of her orgasm, the slow ebb of it through her, as long as she could. She held her breath, but she also held on to every other sensation in her body for a few seconds longer.

'Oh Tim,' she cried hoarsely, contracting around him rhythmically, his own movements speeding.

She felt him release in her. His own desire spurting up inside her, meeting her halfway. The anger and the desire of earlier mingled and passed gradually away, its purpose served for the both of them.

She dropped her legs to the floor, feeling an ache in their backs. Tim's breathing slowed and she smoothed her hands over his rear and he withdrew from her.

'We can't go back down yet,' Tim whispered.

'Too right,' she replied, dropping to her knees.

Chapter Eight

THE PHRASE 'WHEN in Rome, do as the Romans do' held little importance to Andrea King. The times she had been there, which were several, she always did much as she pleased.

DRA had a special relationship with Rome. Its reputation was for being ground-breaking and creative when it came to the launch or branding of European products in other European locations, especially Britain. It was able to take the panache and channel it into the right form to make it successful in the UK. Despite Jerome chiding her at dinner the previous night that she was on nothing more than a glorified shopping spree, she knew that what she had to do was important. Not that it would prevent her having some fun.

In Rome, DRA had a casual relationship with an indigenous design company called Sandros. They provided each other with information and informal help. Nothing was expected and there were no major pressures with the arrangement. It was a business association and to the mutual benefit of all concerned.

Andrea and her contact at Sandros, Philip, had

the same casual relationship with each other. They met, talked business, had fun and fucked. Neither of them exerted pressure and it was a mostly physical situation with a bit of flirtation thrown in. She saw him three, sometimes four, times a year and it suited the both of them fine. Nothing too heavy and no strings.

Philip might in some circumstances have been what her friends and she herself often referred to as 'the one'. He was forty-one years old and divorced, had a son who was ten and was still on good terms with his ex-wife. As far as Andrea could tell, Philip came from old money and did not have to work. He either had a lot of money or stood to inherit a lot when the relevant person died.

Six feet tall and with hair that was midway white to grey and brushed casually backwards over his forehead. Philip was a magnetic figure with a charisma that drew people in, men and women. His face had skin that had seen the weather of time and lines showed around his eyes and at the corners of his mouth. When he smiled, his teeth would show pearl-like and his eyes would somehow change, holding and staring in a way that was intimate and deep but not in an invasive way. Rather, they held Andrea in a warm and protective manner.

She realised that people around her on the plane had stood up and were queuing in the aisles to exit, and was jogged from the pleasant thoughts of Philip. She was only staying over in Rome for one night, for a meeting with a clothes maker about to launch a cologne for men which Andrea hoped they would be able to promote simultaneously in Europe. She had some ideas she thought would interest them. She also wanted to check out a few of the shops and see what was new, what was the current vogue and she wanted to pick something nice up for Tim. Something sexy. Something to say thanks for the nice time in the bathroom at Deanna's house.

Julie, her assistant, had asked whether or not Andrea wanted a room reserved. She told her she did not. Andrea assumed that she would stay with Philip at his apartment near the Piazza di Spagna. Failing that, she would check into a hotel herself.

Coming out of the arrivals gate, she checked her watch and looked around for the driver that Sandros would have laid on for her. They had set up the meeting with the clothing firm, Lazzo, and she had arranged to meet Philip at a small bar nearby, a half hour before the meeting, to give them time to discuss how they should proceed.

She saw a piece of white card with KING in large, neat capital letters. Holding the card and wearing a beaming smile was Philip.

Kissing him, she said, 'Have Sandros got you driving for them now? A demotion?'

'Please,' he smiled, taking her hand and squeezing it before looking at it and planting a gentle kiss on it, the brush of his lips warm against her soft skin.

He took her overnight bag from her, and she put her arm through his as he led her through the lounge. He was wearing a green linen two-piece suit and a brilliant white cotton shirt.

'I thought we were going to meet in that bar round the corner?'

'I know. I asked the driver to stop by my apartment early so I could journey out here and meet you. We still have the limousine. Come, this way.'

81

The limousine was a Mercedes, the sort with three doors down each side. The windows at the back section were blacked out. The driver nodded at her politely as he took her bag from Philip and placed it in the boot. He wore a uniform with a peaked cap.

'This isn't the usual Sandros car,' she half whispered to Philip.

'You must forgive me. I hired it especially. I know we don't have too much time this trip, but I thought it would be nice to be chauffeured around for a while at least.'

She smiled at him and kissed him on his cheek. The driver opened the door for them and they disappeared inside the cavernous interior of the car.

'How have you been?' he asked her, the car moving silently and solidly through the airport traffic.

'Very good. Very good indeed. You know me.'

He laughed. 'Oh yes. I know you. Is business good?'

'Business is, work isn't. You know.'

'Yes. I was sorry to hear about you and Martin.'

She looked at him, her face questioning.

'He called me, business you understand, but I asked him about you, as I always do. He said the two of you were not seeing each other. So you are free again?'

'I'm always free, Philip. I'm seeing someone from work. Off and on.' She left equal short pauses between her sentences. This time he looked at her with a question in his expression.

'His name is Tim and he's nineteen years old. He works for the planning department.'

'As long as he makes you happy, Angel.'

Andrea smiled at him and his first usage of his

favourite name for her. She put her hand on his.

'That's not to say we shan't have our fun, Philip.'

'Why of course not,' he said, acting as though the thought mortified him.

For the next ten minutes they rode in silence, familiarising themselves with each other, the feeling of occupying a common space with someone. Andrea kept her hand on Philip's and it struck her that they were like two lovers riding home in a taxi, coming back from a date. But it was only nine-thirty in the morning. She took the measure of him, sitting passively next to her but still exuding a spell over her, even though he was saying or doing nothing.

She let her hand slip from his and fall on to his leg. She could feel the muscled outline of his thigh against the crumple of the linen. They were separated from the driver by a window and she knew he would not be able to hear them. If he were a professional driver, he would understand discretion. She moved her hand a little further up and let it fall casually between Philip's legs.

He smiled at her, the light of the early morning sun changed by the tint on the windows. He turned towards her and the sun lit him from behind and it traced a halo round his features. She felt for him. She was excited, but she did not at that moment want sex with Philip. She felt comfortable and secure, cossetted in the limousine, her hand resting on him.

By late afternoon, her feelings had changed. She was ready.

The meeting at the clothing firm had been interesting and productive. After a few more moments of silence in the limousine, they had switched into a business gear. Papers rustled and notes were taken. They had spoken several times on the phone about the account and their preamble had the effect of polishing it.

The head of the firm, Old Man Lazzo she imagined his underlings would call him, had the word 'magnate' stamped all over him. Two other junior staff members were present and Andrea managed to strike the right balance with all of them. Philip had told her in the limousine that the boss was big on music, especially classical. That was why the fragrance would be called Symphony. She had got the biggest glimmer of interest from him when she mentioned that 'Rendition' would be a good name for the planned update to the fragrance. They could push it as though he were the composer of the fragrance. She would be able to go back to London and say she had accomplished something. The beginnings of a suitable campaign had already seeded in her mind. She would send out a call report and then convene a meeting of the relevant departmentals.

She and Philip had lunch together in a small restaurant off Corso Vitorio Emanuele. Protocol would normally have involved buying the client lunch, but Lazzo had made it clear that he already had a lunch meeting set up. He had been in the business long enough not to be able to be bought for the price of a lunch. So they were able to have lunch on their own – a bonus. It was a restaurant she had not been to with Philip before, but the staff all seemed to know him well enough. For all she knew, he may have owned the place. That would not have surprised her. She realised she knew so little about this man other than what he had communicated to her, verbally and physically.

At one point during lunch, he excused himself to

go and say hello to a client or friend on another table and she watched him. When Philip stood, his full height slowly unfolded and he took relaxed yet confident strides across the room. He leaned down towards the man at the table, towering over him, and placed his hand on his arm. Several words were exchanged and smiles followed. Andrea sat across the restaurant and gazed at him, appreciating the figure he cut and the charisma, visible even from that distance. He created a space in her that only he himself could fill. This was his charm, she decided. He was attractive purely in and because of himself. He made no demands on her imagination and there was no need to mould him into something else. He was what he was and it suited her fine.

'Well Angel, I think it is time we went around some shops.'

She grinned at the only man in the world she would let call her an Angel. She took care of the bill and they left.

It was just after four and the Rome sunshine was at the point in the day where it was past its intensity and starting the descent into the afternoon proper. It was her favourite time of the day wherever she was, but Rome amplified it for her. The hazy bustle of people and cars, all speeding around in a maniacal way, actually made her feel relaxed. She was always able to relax when she was there, the rest of the city acting as a contrast to her own mood.

The driver dropped them near the Piazza di Spagna, close to Philip's apartment and the major shopping drags of via Condotti and via dell Babuino. Philip told the driver to pick them up at six, checking with Andrea that this would give them enough time.

'What time is your flight out in the morning?' Philip asked her.

She told him her flight time and Philip instructed the driver that he would also need to be at his apartment in the morning in time to get Andrea to the airport. The driver nodded and Andrea wondered what he was thinking. She was glad that she would stay with Philip this trip, even if it was only one night. Some trips, they had used hotels. With another man she would have taken the fact he had not discussed where they would be staying as some sort of mind game. With Philip, it was like everything else – done in a relaxed and confident way without being presumptuous or overbearing.

They looked in the obvious shops, exploring the windows before venturing inside, commenting on displays and the products themselves. Inside the shops they pointed out to each other campaigns that they knew something about. She bought some underwear for Tim which Philip picked up and eyed with surprise, saying it made him feel his age. Once or twice, Andrea made notes in the slim leather organiser she carried in the pocket of her jacket.

The sun which had a few hours earlier begun its wane now dropped gently over the Roman landscape. Andrea and Philip watched it from the crest of the Villa Borghese. The driver had rendezvoused with them and drove them as far up as he could. They stood hand in hand, the cool wind catching Andrea's hair and raising it gently. The Vatican was visible in the distance. The whole criss-cross and multi-level layout of Rome was at her feet. She took a deep breath and it came out as a long sigh. Philip looked at her, as though worried.

'Are you all right, Angel?'

She squeezed his hand in hers and realised her craving for him was growing. She was hungry and greedy and needed to be fed.

'Let's make love,' she said to him.

Less than fifteen minutes later she was in his apartment. She had thrown her jacket on to a chair in the hall and was now standing at the bedroom window, looking out. She opened the window, the air rushing in and then she half closed the brown slatted shutters, obscuring the view of the courtyard below into a small gap between the blinds.

She heard him enter the room but did not turn. Instead she remained facing the window, the last of the sun finding its way through the crack and on to her face. He was behind her quickly, hands on her shoulders. She felt the weight of them bearing down on her. His arms wrapped around her and hugged her close to him. She extended her neck as he ran a hand through her hair, brushing her ear.

As he buried his face in her hair and nuzzled the back of her neck, she shivered. He kissed her nape and then nibbled on one of her ears, the feeling of his teeth surprisingly sharp. His firm hands lifted her blouse and then caressed her stomach. His palms flattened against her taut abdomen and she was conscious of how large he was. When he ran his hands up and under the tight hem at the bottom of her bra, she felt him press into her, a hardness through the linen of his trousers evident against her rear.

Still at her neck, he unclasped her bra under her blouse and she felt herself spill from it. She felt free and careless standing in Philip's bedroom in Rome, the cool current of air wafting at her and his hands roaming under the soft silkiness of her blouse and against her even softer and silkier skin. Expertly, his hands came out of her blouse and reached around her front to the buttons, undoing them. He removed her blouse and her bra before he turned her around.

As he held both her hands, she looked at him. He had taken off his jacket and was now wearing just the brilliant white shirt and the green linen trousers. He had turned the cuffs up on the shirt to reveal tanned forearms with golden hair. At the end of these powerful arms, his square and solid hands cradled hers as though they were delicate pieces of china.

Andrea could hear the silence in the room. There was a stillness and calm that had an undertow of tension and desire. Philip unzipped her skirt and it fell to the floor. She stepped out of it, taking a step nearer to him and the bed as she did so. Now she was in just her lacy knickers with their matching suspender belt and cool, sheer stockings. He removed her knickers.

Philip ran his hands under the straps of the belt at the front of her thighs. His hands in such a suggestive area made Andrea shuffle itchily. His face was turned down towards her crotch and he looked intently, his hair falling forward, a slight wave in it from its length. She reached out and stroked it whilst he rubbed the backs of his hands against the front of her thighs.

'Go and lie down,' he said to her softly, removing his hands from under the suspender straps.

She lay on the large bed. He left the room and she waited, anticipating; desire whispering inside her.

Returning, he placed a small jar on the bedside table.

He went to the chair near the window and sat down on it. He unlaced his shoes and took them off. He placed a sock into each of them and stowed them under the chair. Standing, he unbuttoned his shirt and hung it over the back. Andrea raised her head to watch him, a quiver going through her as she observed the ritualised and poised manner in which he undressed himself, happy with himself and his hard, mature body. He folded the linen trousers and placed them on the seat. His underwear he threw carelessly on to the floor, the first sign of impatience and want in him.

Andrea sat up to see him approach the bed. He was as she remembered, better perhaps. His body was rugged and defined, like a mountain climber. The smooth sleekness of the linen had hidden the robust frame beneath. His cock hung long and hinted at his lust for her. It swung as he made the few steps to the bed. She recalled the size of it when aroused, the hugeness of it and the depths to which it had penetrated her in the past and would do again, soon.

Mounting the bed and her in almost the same movement, he was on top of her and kissing her. She opened her legs to allow him to kneel between them. He towered over her and kissed her, exploring her with his mouth and tongue. After a day of being close to him, she suddenly realised how much closer and intimate this was. A flush was all over her body, every area was sensitive to him and his touch, not just the usual ones. He pushed his hand under the front of the suspender belt, just above her pubic hair and she groaned with pleasure, his hand so near and yet so far from the source of her appetite.

Philip reached for the jar and unscrewed the

lid. He knelt up on the bed and dipped his fingers in. The coldness of it was made more pronounced by the hotness of her clitoris. He spread it around her clit and then between her lips, allowing his finger to probe her a fraction before pulling back. She moved her legs and felt the strings of the suspender belt tighten against her thighs. Gradually, the cream mounded up on her until she was covered in a cold blanket of it.

It was a layer of cold between them. And somewhere in the icy covering, she felt his warm tongue. Through the cool mass it came, searching for her hot clitoris and wanting to push further into her hot pussy beneath. The cream warmed up in her, going from cold to lukewarm to a heat that matched her own. His tongue slavered at her, the cream acting as a lubricant. She heard the noises, the hungry sounds of his mouth making contact with her.

She reached and held the brass bedstead above her, gripping it tightly and pulling her whole body a fraction up the mattress. He continued to work away at her, his white hair falling against her stomach, tickling it as it touched her there. She drew her legs further up and let her knees fall apart, opening herself wider to him, coaxing him to enter her. She wondered what state his cock was in.

It was not long before she found out. He came up, his face smeared, and kissed her. She tasted the strawberry mingled with herself as an aftertaste. Gently sucking his tongue, she felt its warmth and the roughness of its tip, recognising it from its recent visit to her pussy. She looked into his eyes, the magnetism there, drawing her in like a tractor beam. It would take her deep into him and into herself. She felt his pull and was ready to go with him.

Philip reached down and held himself. She watched his hand as he readied himself, the veins in his cock and his forearm standing out equally proudly. He squeezed his cock and it palpitated in his hand, the shaft drumming a low beat. Andrea took the measure of it, its size and circumference. Of the many men she had been with, Philip was the largest in almost every sense. It was not something that worried her in ordinary circumstances. With Philip, his size added to the intensity of the experience. It was part and parcel of him, his worldliness. She never discussed it with him. He probably didn't even realise.

She sat up on the bed and Philip reared up on his knees. She opened her mouth wide and felt the stretch at its corners as the tip of Philip's cock entered her. She knew he did not make a play about being sucked and she did just enough to bring him up to full size, although she wondered why she did. With his shaft in her mouth, reaching to the back of her throat, she was still able to hold its base with her hand. She idled around it, titillating and caressing it with her mouth.

Withdrawing from her mouth, Philip guided her back down on to the bed. Her mouth felt stretched even from such a short encounter with his now rigid cock. He positioned himself between her open legs, his cock close to her lips. He held her by the ankles and pushed her knees up. She rested her feet on his shoulders and she felt the shift inside herself, her vagina ready to be delved into by Philip.

He was careful with her. He opened her slowly and deliberately, the head of his cock parting her lips and finding her opening with precision. With

91

the same definite movement he carried on through and up inside her. He moved like a piston, relentless and heavy. She clenched her eyes shut and her teeth together, a hiss escaping her.

The size of Philip's cock was out of scale, all proportion to what she was used to. It made the act seem different, new and dangerous as though he might literally bore her away to nothing. She felt more consciously aware of the shape of her vagina than she ever did with anyone or anything else. This was real living, breathing and throbbing skin buried in her.

And it did more than simply stretch her. It mined her, going to a depth that caused her to cry out his name and grip him tightly as he supported her hips. It found places deep in her that had never been explored.

Filled with his length and expanded by his width, she lay with her legs up and feet resting on his shoulders. The suspenders were stretched across her legs and the stockings she wore sizzled against her skin. He began to thrust in and out of her. It was more a movement back and forth inside her, rubbing against her and fanning the flame before he would douse it. His lunges moved her whole body with their power as she was opened wide and he pushed still further into her as she gradually relaxed herself. He held her buttocks in his hands, his knees spread on the bed, and he rocked himself into her.

He looked at her and she saw encouragement in his eyes as he lifted her up and moved his hands to grip her thighs on the border of her stockings, bringing his knees closer together. She moved her legs from their bent position until they were up straight against his chest and shoulders.

Letting her thighs stay open, she made herself looser and he now made short, shallow strokes into her. The effect was paralysing, the suddenness of the hasty yet concise jabs anaesthetized her. She was a tingling mixture of nerve endings that were being pushed to their limits. Still he continued in the same fashion, his breathing becoming heavy and his grip on her tighter.

She brought her thighs together, gripping more tightly on his wide cock, causing him to grunt. She wanted him to come and she wanted to come too. She closed her thighs and clutched the walls of her vagina as much as she could around his shaft. The force of his onslaught pinned her to the mattress and the bed sagged and creaked under their combined movement and weight.

Her orgasm was heavy, as if it had fought its way out of her. She was overcome by it and by its cause – Philip. It was almost claustrophobic, having such a large cock embedded in her, forced into such a tight space that she had made tighter by squeezing him with her muscles. And through all of that, she was coming, the orgasm cascading through her, running over her senses. It made her acutely aware of each feeling and sensation.

She held him deep in her and felt him ejaculate, the thundering force of it. She moved her hands around his body and looked at him as he came, still in the mists of her own pleasure.

'Oh Angel,' he said, juddering the last of his come into her.

They held each other for almost an hour. He stayed inside her for most of the time and they lay side by side, her legs wrapped around his waist. She heard the sounds of Rome through the crack in the shutter, the city going into a different gear again, making ready for the evening. Philip was sleeping and she looked at him, brushing the side of his face. She felt the weight of him against her leg and she hugged him tightly.

When she awoke it was early evening. She lay on her side with her back to Philip. He had fitted himself to her shape and was hugging her back, his dormant cock flopping against her rear. One hand was under her neck like a pillow and the other around her waist, his hand resting in her pubic hair. Inside of herself, she felt where he had been. She rolled around to look at him. He was awake.

They kissed.

'What time is it?' she asked him.

He reached over her and picked up the small clock on the bedside table.

'Seven-thirty, almost. Are you hungry?'

'Not yet,' she said, pulling him closer to her and picking up on the warmth of his spent body. 'Let's lie here for a while longer.'

She exhaled heavily, the breath coming from the depths, surprising her with its weight and the feelings it conveyed.

'What?' he said simply.

'Nothing. I don't want to spoil the moment talking about work, like it's always on my mind.' She wondered if he knew about what was happening at DRA. He was well connected, but she did not know if he was close to Carl Anderson. She trusted Philip, but it did not seem that at that moment she should mention anything about what had happened on MCC2. She would tell him about the Creative Director position in due course.

'Don't worry, Angel. Tell me what it is about.'

'There's crap at work right now. Someone new. Not that new, I suppose. She's been on board for a couple of months now. Gillian Kay. Has anyone mentioned her?'

He shook his head and released her, raising himself up on an elbow to look at her. She continued, rubbing his arm with her hand as she spoke.

'I think they've brought her in so they can get rid of me. She came over from Goldman Miller on a really good package. She's no good. Lots of luck, a few successes.'

'They value you too highly, Angel. They would never let you go.'

'Who ever knows how highly you're valued? You only know when you're not. You're out of a job.'

'Can you not work with Gillian? Neutralise her as a threat?' he asked.

'She can't stand me, Philip. We've been enemies for years.'

'And you cannot work things out with Martin? He might be able to do something.'

She shook her head, a wistful smile on her face.

He frowned for a moment and then said, 'What about using Carl Anderson? Can't you get to him?'

'He's too powerful, Philip. The A at the back of DRA? You'd need to do something major to get noticed by him. I'd be just another account manager to him. He's aware of some of my stuff but ultimately I'm faceless.'

'Perhaps I can push you in the direction of your coup. Something to get you noticed.'

After several moments of silence she said to him, 'Well. Don't go strong and silent on me now, Philip. What do you mean?'

'You've heard of Max Ruga?'

'Sports shoes. From Italy originally. They had a famous line in the late-sixties but they fizzled out of sight. Some scruffy bands wear them and it's caused a second-hand market to develop. It's almost like a black market. Kids in London actually buy the original shoes from second-hand shops and markets.'

'Very good. He may be thinking of a re-launch. A new version of the famous shoes and possibly some other sports clothes. He's been practically a recluse for the last fifteen years. I hear through a friend that they are serious about this. He would be a dream come true. If you could bring him out of hiding, sell him in the right way.' He paused. 'It would show Benetton a thing.'

'And, supposing Ruga is going to launch a line, what makes you think DRA or more specifically, I, have a chance of handling it?'

'Well, you have a start on everyone else. This information is from a very close source. Also, he likes Englishwomen. Both his wives were English. One divorced him, the last died tragically. That was when he went into hiding. Do some homework. He's based out of Milan and Nice mostly these days although he travels. It might help. Get you noticed.'

She heard him accent the words delicately in the last two sentences. She let the idea plant itself in her mind as she reached for him.

Chapter Nine

ANDREA SETTLED HERSELF back into the shiny leather seat of the black taxi. The plane from Rome had landed almost an hour ago, but she felt like she was still flying. It had been an exhilarating and useful trip. The Lazzo account had good prospects. Philip was in fine form. And she had been given the jump on Max Ruga. If she could clinch that, DRA would remember why they paid her so much. As part of the overall war of position that would surely ensue until a name was announced for the Creative Director, chasing and bagging Ruga would be a way to demonstrate her abilities at the highest level. The revenue potential from the Ruga account would be phenomenal. They would be able to use all forms of media, the client spend would be enormous. It could easily become DRA's biggest account.

The weather in London was sunny and breezy, as the pilot had said it would be. She had not had a chance to call Tim while in Rome. Was he still a bit pissed off at her over the thing with Jerome at the dinner party, she wondered? She checked her watch and reset it to London time. Ten-thirty. He should be in the office by now, she thought, pulling her portable phone out of her attaché case and recalling DRA from the memory.

'Tim Matthews,' she said when the phone was answered, catching sight of the driver looking up into the rearview mirror and at her. Thom Hall answered.

'Thom, it's Andrea. Is Tim there?'

The taxi sped into the middle lane as they overtook someone.

'What do you mean, sick? Was he in yesterday? Thom, transfer me to Julie please.'

Andrea waited and wondered what Tim was playing at. Perhaps he was licking his wounds. She thought their session in the bathroom at Deanna's house would have pacified him. What was he up to?

'Julie, can you get me Tim's home number and address? It should be on my card file, the one locked in the bottom left drawer of my desk.'

After a few moments, Julie was back on the line with the information Andrea wanted. She leaned forward in the taxi and spoke to the driver through the small gap in the sliding window, giving him a new set of directions.

Thirty-five minutes later, Andrea was outside Tim's house. More precisely, his parents' house. She had thought about calling him but decided against it. Instead, she called Julie back and said she would be in later on in the day and that she should reschedule her meeting with Gillian Kay to tomorrow.

She carried her overnight bag and her attaché up the drive, noting there were no cars parked there. Good. The house was large and detached, but had been built in the last fifteen years, she could tell. It was the sort of comfortable new affluence she would have expected Tim to spring from. She rang the bell and waited.

Tim appeared wearing only a t-shirt and a pair of grey towelling jogging shorts.

'Andrea,' he said, sounding surprised and as if he was asking a question. 'What are you doing here?'

She looked down at her overnight bag and smiled. 'I haven't come to move in, Tim, if that's what you're worried about.' She looked at his legs, sprouting from the loose grey of the shorts, muscular and virtually hairless.

He did not speak.

'I called in for you at work and they said you were off sick, although you look all right to me. Aren't you going to ask me in?'

Tim shifted on his feet and seemed to look over her shoulder as though he were worried someone would see them. Without saying anything, he moved to one side to allow her in. Only when he had closed the door did she speak to him again.

'God, you're looking shifty. Are you up to something?'

He looked embarrassed and she realised he was. She smiled.

'What, have you got a girlfriend here or something?' she said, moving towards him and kissing him, noticing how light the material of the white shirt was.

'Don't be stupid, Andrea. How was your trip?'

'Change the subject if you want. It was very worthwhile. I've bought you some things. If you show me into your living-room, I might give you them.'

Again he looked suspicious, but showed her the way. The room was tweedy and safe in the way she expected it to be. Not unlike her own

mother's house. That was definitely what it was –
a mother's house. No male touches. Sitting on the
sofa, she fished in her overnight bag and
produced two packages and handed them to Tim.
He opened the first.

'It's a new one,' she explained as he looked at
the aftershave. 'We might do the campaign for it.
It isn't out over here yet. Try it.'

He sprayed himself and opened the second
package, holding a pair of briefs up. They both
laughed at the box.

'We definitely need to do these,' said Tim.

'Aren't you going to try them on?'

Casually he stood and pulled off his shorts. He
wasn't wearing any underwear. She saw that his
cock was full and hanging heavy between his
legs. He stepped into the briefs and pulled them
up. They fitted around him perfectly and he filled
them tightly, his crotch bulging and swelling
through the fabric. Tim looked at his watch.

'Tim, are you expecting someone? Is that it?
Shall I leave?' she said in an even voice.

'It's not like that, Andrea. My friend Paul is
coming over, that's all. He's promised to bring a
video. A porn video, actually.' He looked
shamefully at her.

'Is that what you get up to in your spare time?'
she said, a tone of mock horror in her voice. 'I
think I should be going.'

'I don't want you to go. I would call Paul, but he
should have been here by now. I thought it was
him when you rang the bell.'

She was about to reach for him, for his crotch,
hard and defined by the material of the briefs,
when the bell rang.

'Saved by the bell,' she smiled.

For a moment they looked at each other and

then both of them laughed conspiratorially.

'I'll go get rid of him, I promise,' said Tim.

'Make sure he leaves the video behind.'

'Andrea . . .'

'I'm joking, Tim. But get rid of him. I want sex. Now.'

'I could just not answer the door.'

'Go answer the door, Tim,' she said as the second ring came.

'Okay, but you wait next door in the kitchen, just in case. Paul can be hard to get rid of.'

The bell rang a third time and then came the sound of a door knocker.

'He's keen,' said Andrea.

The next thing Andrea heard, from where she stood in the kitchen, was the sound of a voice, not Tim's.

'I've brought it,' the voice said.

Through the gap in the door jam, she saw Paul. He looked older than Tim and was taller. He had short black hair and was slim. Not scrawny, but lean and attractive. At once, she heard her heart beat in her chest and the blood rush about in her ears. Something about the situation appealed to her and held out promise.

For five or ten minutes she listened in on their conversation, following its slow and certain track. Somewhere in the middle of it, the video had been put into the machine. Andrea moved about behind the door in order to get a view of the television screen. The conversation between Tim and his friend Paul had turned to sex early on. Typical talk, nothing that surprised her. She was more excited by the fact of overhearing their words than the words themselves. She was entranced.

'So what's this Andrea like?' Paul asked Tim.

Her ears latched on to the sound of her name and brought her to attention, lifting her from the dreamlike state of a peeping tom.

'She's really nice. Horny.'

'Dirty?'

'Oh, yeah.'

Andrea smiled.

'What sort of things do you do?'

'Everything. Anything.'

'Does she suck you off? All the way off?'

'Yeah.'

There was a silence while this was obviously being considered. Andrea's hand fluttered over her crotch, her palm brushing the material and feeling the tingle it caused, on palm and pussy.

'Does she do that?' Paul said, referring to the television.

On the screen a woman was easing herself down on to a man's cock. The man lay on his back with his legs up towards his chest. His cock was bent down and the woman sat on to the backs of his legs. The man was calling out as much in pain as in pleasure.

'If I want,' replied Tim.

'I'd like that,' said Paul. 'An older woman to give me a good seeing-to. Is she the first?'

'No.'

Andrea listened hard.

'Who was then?'

'Miss Read,' Tim replied without missing a beat or sounding in the least flustered.

'Miss Read? Art? You liar.'

'Do you remember when we were in our last year in the Sixth Form, we had that leavers' disco and I helped her make all the decorations?'

'Yeah.'

Andrea's hand was up under her skirt and

down the front of her knickers, roaming the hot and steamy depths.

'She asked me to help her take them all down.' She kept going on and on about how lovely they were and that she wanted to save them, to use again. After we'd taken them down, she offered me a lift home. She stopped off at her house and we sat in her car for a little while. I sort of knew what she wanted to happen but I didn't know what to do.

'She put her hand on my hair and played with it. She asked me if I wanted to go into her house with her. I think she might have actually asked me if I wanted coffee.' Tim snorted.

Andrea traced a finger along her downy lips, alighting on her clitoris and teasing herself. She felt a rush of blood down below and her clitoris start to swell in her wet lips. Slowly and without a rush, she dipped her hand into a warm and familiar place. A place of safety. With her middle finger, she opened herself and ran the finger slightly out and up her slit, coming to concentrate on her clitoris.

'The next thing I knew, she had my trousers off and we were on the floor in her front room. We did all sorts of things. It was only that one time and we seemed to be trying to cover everything in the one night. I didn't sleep hardly at all and I was sore for a week afterwards.'

Andrea held her breath in an attempt to stifle the sound of her orgasm. Her knickers were damp from her juices and her hand was tired from the quick going-over she had given herself. She needed more than was available in the kitchen.

Twenty minutes later, Tim's briefs and t-shirt

were discarded on an armchair. As she lowered her mouth on to Paul's long, sturdy cock, he too was naked, balanced against the front of the sofa. His legs were splayed out in front of him and Andrea knelt in between them.

When she had made her casual entrance, she thought Paul was about to jump out of his skin. At first, but not for long, he had been angry. Then he picked up on the atmosphere in the same way Andrea had earlier on. She had stripped him off silently and slowly, running her hands over his lean body, feeling his bones and the light pads of muscle that covered him. He had stared at her silently the whole time she was stripping him. His skin was dark but smooth and she relished its feel. His cock had sprung free when she removed his underwear and she wanted to suck on it. It was suckable. She made him sit on the sofa while she quickly removed her own clothes. She saw the look of expectation and passion in his eyes, mixed with nerves. Tim sat to one side, on the arm of one of the chairs, fascinated by what was about to happen.

The two friends had been apprehensive at first, about being naked and sexual in front of each other, Andrea could tell. But now, their inhibitions were ready to drop, or failing that, be pushed over by her.

She pushed Paul's foreskin and he leaned back on the sofa and closed his eyes. He tasted bitter on her tongue and the head of his cock was hot. The phallus was large and it plugged her mouth as she let it go past her lips and into the cavity. She closed her lips on the shaft and moved her head back, allowing the glans to drag out over her lips until he was no longer in her mouth. Gently and carefully, she repeated the action several times, Paul gasping a little more with each stroke.

Letting his cock recover from her mouth, she masturbated him quickly, the cock rigid and still in her hand. She enjoyed using the foreskin, sheathing up and down his shaft and moulding it around the head of his cock as she pulled upwards. The head was shining, covered in fluid. Her pussy was sweltering away, almost as if sweating from exertion. It ached to be filled.

Paul moved his hips up, directing his cock back towards Andrea's mouth. She received and set to work on it in earnest. She took in the length of the cock, top to toe and out again. It rolled and moved in her mouth and Andrea ran her hands over Paul's thighs and tickled his balls with her fingernails.

Conscious of Tim moving, she wondered what he was up to. She soon found out. He lay down with his back on the floor and slid himself under her, so his face was directly under her pussy. She felt his breath on it. His hands held her rear and gently eased her down. She made contact with his face and the sensation was glorious, his tongue immediately lapping away at her, flicking about in her most sensitive areas with little regard for finer feelings. She was being tongued quickly and efficiently and she wiggled on Tim's face, trying to open herself to him.

In her mouth, Paul's cock remained upright and sturdy. As it had grown harder, she was aware of a slight curve along its top. While Tim had been licking her, she had been on autopilot with Paul's young virgin cock and she told herself that for now at least she would concentrate on it. She wanted his first blowjob to be a memorable one, even if it didn't feel like it was going to be an especially long one.

The pace of her mouth over Paul's cock was echoed by Tim and his tongue down underneath her. She thought they must have looked like some sort of machine if they had been viewed from a distance. Paul with his cock deep in Andrea's mouth, Tim eating her pussy. An efficient machine, each giving someone else pleasure, moving in an orbit at different speeds but all pushing in the same direction. Their individual sounds – sighs, whimpers and groans – touching different corners of the room.

Andrea expected to be the first to come. She was surprised when she heard Paul give a cry and his body began to move erratically, as though trying to go off in different directions at once. His cock pulsed in her mouth, the shaft of it expanding in circumference as she literally felt the first wad of spunk travel along him. He cried out as he ejaculated into her mouth. Andrea kept on flicking her tongue, concentrating on the tip of his cock as there came another four equally spaced spasms.

The hot come gathered in her mouth and she took a breath through her nose before carefully swallowing it without taking his cock from her mouth. Paul tensed, pushing his stomach upwards as his orgasm continued to hold him in its grip. Andrea held on to the base of his cock and continued to lick and mouth it, bringing him down slowly and turning her attention to where Tim was.

She let Paul slip from her mouth and sat upright, using his knees for support. Paul opened his eyes and looked at her, obviously keen to watch her come. She would give him a good show.

Tim pushed his tongue inside her, through her

lips and into her while he played a hand over her rear, occasionally letting a finger tease around her anus. Andrea rocked backwards and forwards on to Tim's face, his forehead and eyes visible through her legs. She was sweating and it covered her full breasts and moistened the crevice between them. Sweat ran over her stomach and on to the top of her pubic hair. While Tim still had his tongue inside her, she toyed with her clitoris, encouraging it and pleading with it to give her release.

All the while, Paul watched her wide-eyed, his recently spent cock already showing signs of firmness, the last vestiges of his orgasm visible in its occasional quiver.

'Oh!' Andrea cried, grinding faster on to Tim and massaging herself. She let out small screams and shook her hair around as she came in heated bursts not dissimilar to the way Paul had earlier. She clamped her thighs around Tim's face and kept him there, letting him feed from her and drink deep from her, enjoying the sensation of him there while she came. Paul stared on, bug-eyed, as she crushed Tim's face under her.

When she lifted herself from his face, which was covered in her juices and a smile, she turned to look at his cock, pumped up and ready to open her. Still feeling tumult between her legs, she quickly scrambled off his shoulders and sat down on his stomach, feeling his cock press her rear as she did so.

She hopped off him and held his ankles, pushing them up towards his chest. Tim held his legs behind the knees and Andrea reached for his cock and held it so it stood out. Now he was positioned just like the man in the video, the image Paul had found so fascinating.

Andrea stood with her back to Tim and crouched carefully down so that she could sit on the backs of his thighs. Tim's athletic body was easily moulded into position but she instructed Paul to hold Tim's ankles for her, which he did, allowing Tim to grip her wrists and give her more stability.

A shimmering, moist cavity between her legs, her pussy pushed out from behind her as the crouch became a sitting position. She reached down and put him in her. Somewhere in the midst of the heat and desire down there, she felt Tim penetrate her. The hardness of his cock, its rigid stillness, was the perfect counterpart to the bustle of her pussy, opened from underneath and acceptant.

Tim let out a moan, the angle of his cock obviously painful, stretched down between his legs and pointing outwards as though it had grown suddenly from his rear. In her it felt as though it were trying to lever back to its normal position and that it would take her with it.

She was pleased when she freed a hand from Tim's grasp and reached down and found her clitoris so perfectly exposed and ready to be stimulated. She pushed down on Tim's cock until she could see his balls against her pussy lips. She swayed and tottered on him, sighing as she reached down and explored her impaled pussy. She touched around her spread lips, rustled in her pubic hair and eventually touched where she most wanted to. She rubbed away happily, sometimes touching where Tim's shaft was inside her.

'Paul, come on round here, will you?'

In an instant he was there. She held his cock, gently moving it, feeling its heft and weight. Then

108

she carefully squeezed at her clitoris and masturbated herself. He watched her and she looked back at him.

She reached her hands out to him and he knelt and took them, understanding. He held his arms still and Andrea pulled on them, the motion lifting her from Tim's cock and then back down on to it as she released her hold.

Again, she wondered how they must have looked. Tim on his back, knees bunched up to his chest, cock pushed outwards with Andrea sat firmly on it, pushing him in and out of her. In the meantime, the no longer so virginal Paul was pulling on her arms to give her the required momentum to be fucked by Tim. The centre of attention as always Andrea, she thought to herself.

Anchoring herself solidly on Tim, absorbing as much of him as she could, she moved her rear from side to side. His pubic hair tickled her and his cock touched the walls of her vagina as she moved over him in a slow and steady motion, feeling the cheeks of her rear spread from side to side. Tim's feet were against the back of her shoulders. He rubbed her provocatively with the soles, while his hands explored her backside and ran over her lower back. In her pussy, there was an almost hungry feeling as she ascended and descended on Tim's rigid cock.

Gradually she warmed to the invasion. It was a familiar pattern to her, made exciting by the different ways of getting there. She grew to be pliable and as one with the cock. When it first entered her, from whatever direction or angle, it was a stranger to her and she was acutely aware of it and its capability. Now she was at the stage where it became almost a part of her. It was in her and part of the overall scheme of lust and desire. It was integrated into her and she was able to use it to give her pleasure and to give him pleasure.

The video had long since finished and the television was on standby. Sun shone in through the leaded windows of the room and Andrea thrilled at the possibility of someone coming up the drive and spotting them through the window, lost in each other, feasting themselves. The waft of Tim's cologne filled her nostrils as surely as he filled her with himself.

She lifted herself and held the head of his shaft just inside her. She made fast movements that stimulated her at the opening of her vagina and which would also excite Tim. She wanted him to come inside her. He would shoot his semen into her at this odd angle and she would feel it empty in her, touching her and mingling with her own juices.

Paul had tentatively begun masturbating himself with one hand and Andrea with the other. He was kneeling close in and had started on her first. He fiddled and flicked at her clitoris, occasionally touching where she and Tim were joined, quickly moving his hand away again as though he had done something he shouldn't. His hand worked himself expertly, rubbing and squeezing at his cock. Andrea watched it fill with blood and the way he manipulated and pulled at himself, the practised efficiency of the act.

Her lips and the ridges of her sopping vagina continued to hold tight against Tim and she could feel how close he was. She moved quicker and as harshly as her position would allow her to. She made circular movements followed by side to side movements and then back to up and down. She clenched and unclenched her buttocks and she heard Tim growl and felt him shift under her. What would his orgasm be like, she thought, bunched up and bent back the way he was?

He called her name as he shot into her. She rode him and his orgasm as his grip on her wrists increased the pull into him while he pushed against her shoulders with his feet. She was spread out between being pulled in and pushed away, all the while Tim's cock launching fiery come into her.

As soon as he released her wrists, she was off him and on her knees, her hand all over her clitoris. A line of semen drained from her and ran down the hot skin that led to her anus. She opened her knees wider and pushed a finger in where Tim had so recently been, feeling the evidence for herself. Her orgasm was about to spill over and brim from her. She leaned back and Tim, now upright on his knees behind her, supported her, hands under her arms and over her chest.

She quaked in his arms, wrestling in his grip as the orgasm tried to break her free. She felt it hit her and knock her back; waves of bliss bathed her and then she felt the warm shots of Paul, managing a second orgasm on her. His come spurted on to her hand and over her pubic hair. She continued to move her hand as the orgasm washed away like the tide, feeling Tim's come in her and Paul's over her. It was as though she were drowning in it.

Like a Roman statue, they remained frozen in position for minutes, their thoughts and feelings obliterated by sex. She let her hand rest on Tim's and her feelings returned to her.

It was good to be home.

Chapter Ten

IT WAS A relief to get back to the office for a normal day. The previous months had been busy generally and the last week particularly so. The second module of MCC and the announcement of the new senior position had thrown everyone into a spin.

The fact that Carl Anderson himself had gone to the meeting to announce it had added to the effect. The cold and deliberate way in which he had laid it out – he wanted someone for the new role from in house but apart from that, there were no prescriptions. They were not likely to see someone from the post room ending up as Creative Director, but what Anderson had meant, Andrea believed, was that they should not expect an obvious appointment. People who were high in DRA's almost invisible power structure were being warned not to feel too comfortable.

Andrea knew it was a good strategy as it had the effect of keeping everyone on their toes, creating just the right edge. This had been sealed by the merciless way in which a man as nice as Mike Mitchell had been fired. But that was Anderson's way. When most other agency directors got into Buddhism, Carl Anderson took up full contact karate. As a result of the atmosphere, anyone who could be a candidate was busy consolidating their plans and refusing to share anything. Real allegiances and friendships were being tested.

Andrea had gone straight from MCC2 to dinner at Deanna's house in the evening and from there on to Rome the next day. The Lazzo account could be good steady business. She had pondered the approach and the Symphony/Rendition concept and was still happy with it in the cold light of day – providing she could cajole the creatives into thinking it was their idea. She had jotted down some more thoughts and would get Tim to help her work it from the planning side. Tim. She smiled to herself.

Rome had opened up more possibilities than just the Lazzo business. There was Ruga. This, above all other things, had filled her thoughts the most. She was bursting with the secret and knew she could tell no one just yet. Almost no one. The degree of visibility associated with it would be enormous, blinding almost. All the way up to Carl Anderson.

These thoughts occupied her mind in background mode for most of the morning, as she went through her correspondence, made and returned phone calls. She had gone for a minimal look with very little makeup and her hair pulled back save for the few strands she had allowed to fall in her face. Her clothes were equally subdued, though expensive. She wore a simple pair of Donna Karan slacks and an Hermès jacket, much like a riding coat, over a soft wool polo neck.

'Nice to see you back.'

It was Gillian Kay. After Andrea had asked Julie

to reschedule their meeting from yesterday to today, she arrived to find that Gillian's assistant had rescheduled it to tomorrow.

'It's always nice to be back, although it's important to be out there in front of people, drumming up some business. There's no point in letting the furniture get too comfortable,' said Andrea, continuing to work at the papers on her desk.

One of the first rumours that had started about Gillian was her insistence on having her office refitted before she joined DRA.

'I was expecting you back yesterday.'

'I wasn't aware you were expecting anything, Gill,' she came back immediately, managing to shorten her name to the form she knew Gillian hated.

'I thought perhaps you were hiding away. I was going to ask Tim where you were, but then he was out as well yesterday.'

'Tim?'

'Yes, I thought he might know where you were.' Gillian smirked. Andrea wondered when the last time was she'd seen a good fucking.

'Is there something I can help you with, Gill?'

'I wondered if there was any feedback on the Lazzo meeting. We tried dealing with them when I was over at Goldman Miller, but we never got very far.'

'The meeting was successful. I've got a few ideas and some things I want to try out. I'll be giving it to Tim. Later, most likely.' She smiled, watching Gillian assimilate the sentence and its innuendo before she left.

Andrea called Tim on the phone and in a minute or so he was there. She asked him to close the door and sit down.

'Tim, I'm going to let you in on something, okay?'

He nodded.

'This is serious. I'm doing this because I trust you and because I want you to help me, do you understand? This goes no further.'

'What is it?'

'When we were away on the second module of MCC, Carl Anderson turned up and announced out of the blue that he was recruiting in house for a new Creative Director.'

'I know. The rumour factory's been running wild. No one's supposed to know. Apparently someone from *Campaign* called already. Why didn't you tell me when I came to the hotel that night? Or when we were at dinner at Deanna's house?'

'Work was hardly on your mind then, Tim,' she reminded him.

'Have they approached you for the job?'

She smiled. 'Not quite. Anderson's playing with everyone at the moment. He's created the feeling that it could be anyone.'

'When are they going to select someone?'

'Over the next few weeks. I think they'll wait until we've finished MCC and there would be a choice on that basis. I think I have a way to secure it.'

'How?'

'Have you ever heard of Max Ruga?'

He shook his head.

'Before your time, most likely. He designed a range of sports shoes that were popular in the sixties. Onyx, they were called.'

'I know those. I just didn't know he designed them,' said Tim.

'Well, Ruga is apparently thinking of a

re-launch and will be looking for an agency. He's been a recluse for over fifteen years now. My contact thinks he might go for an English agency. I'm trying to work on a line into Ruga but I want some good background before I do. Which is where I need you.'

He looked at her as though he would be willing to do anything.

'You are a very good researcher, Tim. I want you to look into Ruga for me. Anything you think might be useful. It's not even public knowledge that Ruga will re-launch, so when it breaks, we'll have the jump on everyone.'

'This is like insider trading. Is it legal?'

'It's advertising, Tim. You'll have to dig. I don't know much more about him than I've just told you. I'll check back with my contact and we'll go from there, okay?'

'What are you up to tonight?' he asked her expectantly.

'I'll be here late. What about you?'

'Me too.'

'I'll talk to you later then?'

'Sure,' he said, getting up and looking a little crestfallen.

Before he made it to the door she said, 'Tim, how's your friend Paul?'

Tim smiled at her. 'I don't think he'll ever be quite the same again.'

'Talk to you later then.'

She took lunch at her desk and spent the rest of the afternoon with her head in papers or the phone pressed to her ear, sometimes both.

When she next looked up, it was Tim who roused her, tapping gently on the door jam of her office. She smiled at him. He was wearing a beige pair of chinos and a crisp white shirt with the top

116

button fastened. The buttons on his linen waistcoat were also done up. Already, she noticed that his hair was getting long. She thought how appealing he would look if he let the fringe grow.

'It's ten past seven,' he said to her with concern in his voice.

'Is it? It is,' she said looking at her watch. 'Jesus.'

'I've done some work on the Lazzo account and also some stuff on Ruga, but not much. Do you want to talk about it?'

She was about to reprimand him for mentioning Ruga's name aloud when she realised that the office was empty as far as she could see. Little by little, the steady and insistent soundtrack of ringing phones, fax machines, printers, chatter and laughter had faded. Her office was illuminated only by a desk lamp.

'We can talk about it tomorrow,' she said. 'Are you hungry?'

'I'm horny, actually.'

'What do you feel the most, hungry or horny?'

'Definitely the latter.'

'I feel grubby. Let's take a shower.'

They giggled conspiratorially in the lift on the way to the fourth floor. They had cobbled together two towels – one from Andrea's gym bag and another from someone else's. She kissed him as they ascended in the lift. The bump of the elevator arriving on the fourth floor jolted their mouths apart.

'Is this going to be all right?'

'Tim, I'm allowed to use the shower. We all are. That's why it's here.'

'But are we allowed to use it together?' he sniggered.

'Just see it as a way of saving water for DRA. I

bet Martin and Carl Anderson often while away an hour or two in here together.'

She flicked the switch, the fluorescent light rattling into action. The room was Spartan. Cold ridged tiles covered floor and walls with only a rubber slip mat to warm the decor. The shower area was large and had a power shower – very advertising, Andrea always thought.

Under the harsh light, they continued the kiss interrupted by the elevator. She rubbed the fabric of his chinos on his hips and felt his sides, reaching into his now unbuttoned waistcoat. He was wearing the sample of Symphony she had brought him back. She unfastened the button at the top of his chinos and slid his zip down. He stood on the backs of his shoes to lever them off and followed it by pulling his trousers off. She removed the linen waistcoat which weighed light in her hands but felt warm from where it had been against his body. She wanted to feel that warmth radiated to her. While he undid the buttons of his shirt, Andrea fluidly slipped off the slacks, riding jacket and polo neck. She let her hair down.

'Oh, they look good on you,' Andrea said, commenting on the underwear from Rome, which he had worn so briefly yesterday at his mother's house.

She weighed his crotch in her hand, his cock stirring and extending the fabric. The briefs clung to his legs, a small gap appearing where the front of his thigh had a muscular indent. She smoothed her hands all about the underwear before removing it, leaving him naked and erect in front of her.

'Christ!' squealed Tim as a jet of cold water hit him when he turned on the shower. He jumped back from it, his cock swaying from side to side.

'That's why I asked you to get in first,' Andrea

said devilishly as she removed the last of her clothes.

He flicked cold water at her and it hit her icily on the stomach and breasts. She shouted at him and darted towards him in the shower. She lunged for him and flung her arms around him, putting the both of them under the stream of now lukewarm water.

They laughed and kissed, rocking from side to side under the cascade of water. Shower sex was one of the best things next to hotel sex, she thought. In a hotel shower, well that would have been bliss itself. Both her and Tim's hair was wet. She was thankful she had gone easy on the makeup today or else she would have looked like a clown in a storm by now.

Tim's body was young and firm. She knew he liked to work out and that he also cycled a lot. He was finely proportioned, not too heavily built nor too skinny. She gripped different parts of him, exhilarated to be awash with this boy.

'Do you know what I was doing yesterday, while I was listening to you and your friend Paul?' she asked him coyly.

'What?'

She pulled away from him and reached down to her crotch. She found her clitoris and moved it around between her fingers.

He laughed and said, 'You're rude.'

While Tim looked on, she continued to feel herself, the water falling between her and Tim in an even torrent, separating them. She enjoyed the look of his face, the concentration and appreciation as she worked away at herself, a craving in her slowly overtaking her. She wondered how long she would be able to hold out before surrendering to it. Her fingers toiled away, making habitual patterns and movements, ones that she knew would shape her urges and form them into something powerful and pleasureable.

Tim reached for the shower attachment and held it in his hand. Water sprayed off in different directions, spattering against the frosted white curtain. He directed the jet at her breasts, letting the water douse her between them. She felt the warmth and the tingling as the water drummed on to her body. He moved the shower head a fraction closer and the reverberation increased. He moved it around and she felt it on her rib cage. It made her stomach seem hollow as it beat against it, a fast rhythm. Still she continued to finger herself.

Against her hips and then around her back to her buttocks, Tim continued to use the shower attachment over her body, like he was searching her with a metal detector. He sprayed water at the base of her backside where her legs opened at the mouth of her pussy. She felt the water against her perineum, tickling her and gushing on through to where her hand was at her front.

And then it was gone.

Her body was now as wet as her pussy. Tim replaced the shower attachment and squeezed some of the blue shower gel on to the palm of his hands. He rubbed his hands together to get a covering of gel on each and then held her breasts in his hands, smearing the gel over them. The lubricant allowed his hands to slide freely and graze the tips of her nipples which protruded from her. The gel worked itself up into a foam and Andrea's hands left her pussy and she rested both on his narrow hips, moving her head lazily from side to side.

Over her stomach, Tim smoothed the fragrant

gel. He fitted a hand around each of her hips and squeezed them so that she slipped around in his hands, feeling pliable. Her whole body was becoming gradually lubricated. He was priming her with the gel, making her smooth and oiled before he would shatter it with his hardness.

He pulled her buttocks wide as he soaped them and her anus felt exposed and on view, even though he was reaching behind her and could not actually see her there. Suds covered the entire front of her body and now he was waxing over her buttocks with his steady young hands. Soon the palms took on the form of a finger. It toyed at her anus, both timid and teasing at the same time. Then he reached under her, finding her pussy from behind.

It felt as though it needed no oiling, but he poured more gel into his hand and used it to soap up her pussy hair. It soon became foamy and he moved his hand quickly against her lips, not penetrating her, but simply making movements against her. It gave her a feeling of vertigo and she reached out to hold on to him.

Andrea bent over and rested her hands on the small wall that separated the shower area from the changing area. It was seven or eight inches high and you had to step over it to get into the shower. Her breasts hung loosely from her and she curved her open legs to present her upturned pussy to Tim in the most inviting way possible.

He wasted no time. She felt him take up position behind her, his feet brushing her own. Then his cock lit against her legs as he bent in, his own legs fitting in behind hers and imitating their curve. She heard him shuffle his feet as he opened his legs a little wider. One of his hands rested on the small of her back. As the tip of his cock touched the lips of her vagina, she shivered. He must have been using the other hand to guide himself into her. When he was partly inside, his hand disappeared and then they both returned, gripping her hips and positioning her body.

Tim's athleticism and control never ceased to amaze her. She probably had his art teacher to thank for that, she thought to herself. His cock tunnelled into her. She loved being joined to him in this way, the feel of him hot and alive and deep inside her. She liked the way his body would fit against hers and they would share an intimacy and closeness his rigid cock splaying her open.

She used the wall she was resting her hands on to push herself back on to his cock.

'Fuck me, you big bastard,' she said to him, looking over her shoulder at him and wriggling her rear. They both giggled.

Andrea dropped her shoulders lower by bending at the elbows and Tim pushed himself further into her. His cock was against the sensitive front wall of her vagina and she sighed as he started to move in and out of her, enjoying the delayed soft slap of his balls against her buttocks. She reached under and tickled them.

'That's it,' she said to him, trying to give him some encouragement. 'Finger me, Tim.'

He crouched and she felt him reach round. He stimulated her clitoris and managed to keep a low thrust going at the same time. The lather over her body made them slide about together and she wanted Tim to lubricate her inside, to wash through her and rain into her, the same way as the water in the shower.

The force of Tim's lunges jerked her body forward and she grunted like an animal in time with them. She felt like an animal and Tim was pounding at her like one. She wanted him to rut her pussy, to shove her backwards and forwards until they both came. She seethed as he pulled out of her and mined back in.

A slap on her right buttock. Tim's hand, cautious and imploring at the same time. She grunted approval and asked him to do it again, a little harder. Another crack and it stung slightly, just enough to know he had spanked her. Several more spanks rained down on her, each exquisite, creating more of an itch than a pain. The sting translated itself clearly into her pussy which sang out in approval.

Releasing her grip on the wall, Andrea eased her body into more of a bending position, Tim moving his legs to facilitate her shift in posture. The pressure of his cock against her inside was intensified by their new position. She felt as though it had sneaked up on her and was appearing from an unknown angle. She could not see Tim, only feel his hands over her and his cock inside her. She let the sensation of touch take over from her sight. She relied on the sound of him furrowing into her, the pine forest smell of them both covered in the gel.

Tim was deep in her and he moved freely and powerfully, controlling the depth and the speed of his entries into her. Against her insides, at the front, Tim's cock did its work, kindling her orgasm, taking it from a small spark into a flame. Eventually it would become a fire. For now, she was happy for him to fan the flames.

She stood as upright as she could with a cock sunk into her pussy from behind. She felt his wet torso against her back. Her head dropped forward and her hair hung freely down. His hand was back on her clitoris, motioning around and on it.

His other hand was on the back of her head, smoothing through her hair. He bit at her neck and then kissed it. Her buttocks were squashed by his groin as he fucked her. They continued in this posture for several minutes, Andrea and Tim closer to climax by the second.

Arching her back, she moved away from Tim and his cock slid from her. She felt her lips close and the empty feeling it left behind in her vagina. However, her clitoris was still alert and in need of relief. She fell to her knees without looking at Tim and masturbated herself vigorously as the water splashed on to her back. She wriggled and shifted on the tiles, stretching her spine and flicking her head about. She curved her back and presented her rear to Tim.

'Spank me again, Tim.'

He knelt beside her and kneaded her bottom with his hand. She saw his arm move back and felt his hand land flatly against her. Before the feeling had gone right through her, it was back again. And then again. He administered several quick slaps to her rear, all of them careful and well positioned. She shivered despite the heat of her body and water.

Steam had filled the small shower room as she knelt on the floor, bottom in the air being spanked by her nineteen-year-old junior planner. Her pussy quavered of its own accord, out of synchronisation with the rest of her desire. She was going to come.

'Spank me. Come on me,' she whispered to him hoarsely.

As his hand rained down on her, the spanks wet and cracking, she orgasmed with a vengeance. Her juices ran from her as though her body was flushing itself out, emptying her desire.

Her pussy droned and her backside warmed to Tim's hand. She writhed on the floor, her climax was long and low, tugging at her and niggling at all her senses, demanding her full attention and repaying her with an intensity that shook her to her centre.

The spatter of Tim's come on her buttocks was hot and thick. He came in several long jets that managed to cover most of the area he had tanned with his hand. It was soothing on her spanked bottom, to feel his fluid cover her and run over her. He cried out as he came and she knelt there, head almost on the floor, listening to him and feeling him on her.

Her hair was still damp when she arrived home. Sitting in the car, her pussy and her backside had hummed all the way. There was a message on the machine from Philip. She picked up and dialled his number.

'Philip, it's Andrea,' she said when he answered.

'Angel, I think I may have a fix on Ruga for you.'

'Where?'

'How would you like to go to Nice?'

Chapter Eleven

LIKE A SHEET of cool azure, the Mediterranean spread out beneath the plane as it neared the airport. Andrea had flown to Nice several times and on each occasion it had felt as though the sea were about to swallow the aircraft as it made its descent towards it. As usual, the runway appeared as if from nowhere and caught them. The plane bumped gently on to it and went into a noisy reverse thrust.

Nice reminded her of a James Bond film from the sixties, with its dreamy watercolour look. On the descent, even the recycled air in the plane seemed fresh when viewed in time with white buildings etched into the coastline and joined to the turquoise sea by a belt of sand.

It was her own private secret-agent film, she thought. The bright weather, the bustle of traffic, all of it had a filmic quality. Philip had given her the address of a house where Ruga was staying, and she had booked her ticket immediately she got off the phone with Philip. She threw some things into an overnight bag and that morning she called in to say she would be working from home. The rest she would handle when she got back. After she had met with Ruga.

The taxi driver knew exactly where she meant, a relief as she only had to use the minimum of her minimal French. She bounced around in the rear of the taxi as it made its way into the hills, the roads becoming more like dirt tracks the higher they climbed. Fifteen minutes and several hundred francs later, she was standing at the end of the drive to Ruga's house. She had sent the taxi away. She would not need it so soon: she felt lucky.

The house was low and wide, set out on its own with no others nearby. Several heavy pillars at the top of the steps leading to the front door made it look a little like the White House, she thought, as she was halfway up the drive. No cars or people were in evidence. The mid-morning quiet was broken only by the occasional car on the nearby road. A feeling of déjà vu came over her as she remembered her journey to Tim's parents' house in the taxi, and a similar walk up an albeit less impressive driveway.

She braced herself as she climbed the steps, going over what she would say to Ruga. She took even breaths, the same time between inhaling and exhaling, to give her a continuity. She took a single deep breath and rang the doorbell. In almost no time, it was answered.

'*Bonjour. Je m'appelle Andrea King. Parlez-vouz Anglais?*' she said.

'*Oui*,' said the maid, before changing it to, 'yes.'

'I'm here to see Max. He's expecting me.'

She and Philip had decided that the only way to play the situation was for her to appear as though she was expected by Ruga and familiar to him.

'I will go and tell him,' said the maid. She was wearing a traditional, almost stereotypical, uniform, right down to the lacy white hat. She motioned for Andrea to enter and closed the door behind them.

The hall was tiled and had more of a peasant cantina effect as opposed to the kind of plush opulence Andrea had imagined would lie behind the white façade. The maid picked up a phone from a table in the hall and spoke in French, both too quickly and too native for Andrea to follow.

'Please wait here. He will see you in a moment.'

As the maid left, exiting along the hallway, Andrea stood near the door feeling awkward and spare, as if she had come to apply for a job as a chambermaid. She let the fact flow over her that she had made it this far.

'Hello,' said a man's voice from the top of the stairs.

She could only see his feet as he began his descent. They were clad in black Chelsea boots. She waited. When he came into view, she saw a short man, in his late-twenties. He was wearing black jeans and an expensive-looking black t-shirt, most likely Versace.

'Can I help you?' he asked.

'I'm here to see Max,' she said casually.

As he reached the bottom of the stairs, he extended his hand to her.

'As I said, can I help you?' he repeated, clasping her hand. It was delicate, the fingers bony and long. Pianist's hands.

'You're not Max Ruga,' she said.

'I am *a* Max Ruga. It is not very often I am *the* Max Ruga.' He pursed his lips.

Andrea looked at him closely. His lips were full, despite their current pout, and his skin a shade of olive. His eyebrows were heavily set over brown eyes, the lashes long and sensuous. The full cheeks, small ears and shock of brown hair that fell into a floppy fringe looked familiar. She thought of Ruga's photographs – all two of them she had dug out from DRA's research files. Those of his first wife, divorced from him and often photographed. The one of the son and daughter when they would have been ten years old. A picture she had only glanced at. All of this and the man in front of her could only have added up to one thing.

'You're his son?' she asked him.

'Yes. I am *his* son.'

'Is your father here?'

'Right now? No.' He was looking at her closely, his eyes travelling up and down her figure, stopping in the most obvious places. Andrea was familiar with the way men looked at her, but this felt different. He was appraising her deeply. She sensed it in his stare. Something which was more than simply lascivious.

'Business?' he asked her.

'Business,' she replied. 'Do you know if he will be here later?'

'I am not sure.' He raised his shoulders and narrowed his eyes. 'It is possible.' He put his hands into the pockets of his jeans and shuffled his Chelsea boots on the tiles.

'Is there any way you can find out?'

'No.' He was looking at her overnight bag. 'But you can wait for a little while. If that will help.'

She nodded. 'Thank you.'

'You are here to see him on business?' he said again over his shoulder to her as he led her along the hall towards the back of the house.

'Yes, that's right. This is a wonderful house,' she said, veering away from her purpose.

He led her through a small conservatory-type room and out through double doors on to a patio.

The view was stunning. In the far distance, mountains. In her immediate view, an olive grove. The small trees looked like something out of a biblical scene, stretching silently out in front of her and dipping into the small valley. The gentle wind shook the leaves and nets at the foot of each tree cradled the odd fallen olive.

'We only rent this house. Father has several of his own, but this one is his favourite. At this time of year especially. The owner will never sell it, knowing how much he can charge Father for it. And to sell it to an Italian . . .'

Andrea laughed.

'Please,' he said, pointing to the table and chairs. 'I will bring us something to drink.'

She sat and looked out across the grove. For the past few minutes she had completely lost the sense of her purpose for being there. Her disappointment had been quelled by the splendour of the house and the simplicity of the view. She was intrigued by the lonely, wistful charm of Ruga's son, alone in the house apart from the help. She gazed at the sky, the sun climbing high into its centre as noon approached.

Ruga's son returned with a tray. She wondered why he did not ask the maid to bring it. It contained several glasses and two bottles. He set the four glasses down and poured fizzy mineral water into two of them, the bubbles hissing as they made contact with the glass and air. The remaining two glasses he filled with a golden white wine. He set down a bowl of olives. He was wordless, concentrating hard on the task.

'Thank you,' she said, taking a glass of the wine and sipping from it. It had a cool, creamy taste that cleaned her pallet. She picked up an olive and placed it in her mouth, enjoying the oily familiarity and the soft juiciness of the flesh.

For a little while they sat in silence. She felt neither familiar nor foreign to him. She was absorbed in herself and the view; by the wine and the water. He did not seem troubled by the silence. She looked over at him and thought about what she should say to him.

'Do you rent his house every year?' she asked.

'I have been in this house every year that I can remember. Since I was a very small child. There are photographs of me taken here that I cannot remember.'

'Does your mother ever come here?'

He looked at her as if to say she had done her homework. He hesitated for a moment, looking as though he was deciding whether or not to continue. He did.

'No. I see her in other places. She will not come here. Not because of my father. Just because of the house. It is bigger than just her and him – all the things associated with it.'

'Do you work for your father?'

'Yes. And no. It is not work really. I am indulged by him and his generosity. There are many people looking after Father's affairs. I am just a small part of it. You will stay for lunch?' The last sentence blurted out of him, like it had been bottled up and on his mind the whole time.

She sat up in the chair, about to say that she was not sure.

'You must. I have told Anne-Marie already. She will be preparing things. We cannot let her down.'

The sentence came out sounding grasping, as though he were afraid, petrified almost, that she was about to leave. She looked at him.

For perhaps the first time, he smiled. She stared

at him, the sullen, secluded man. Her own age or older, but like a boy in so many ways. He would no doubt have had access to almost unlimited wealth. Certainly enough money to have anything he could want for. At that moment, she sensed what he wanted was for her to stay and have lunch with him. She felt flattered and she felt sympathetic. It was already clear to her that the Max Ruga senior was not going to appear.

'I'd love to,' she said, returning his smile.

They ate lunch in the conservatory, the doors open wide and the wind drafting in softly. Anne-Marie, the maid, had laid the table whilst they had sat on the patio and talked. She had placed several vases of flowers at various places and it made the whole room seem brighter and friendlier. The light from the sun, high in the sky, was diffused by the glass of the room and its intensity was broken down into a delicate sheet that enfolded them as they sat at the table.

'The tulips are wonderful,' she said, looking at the vase on the table. 'Are they grown here?'

He nodded.

About twenty in all, the stems were long with velvety green leaves drooping from them, the ends forming into lazy points. The base of the stems were tightly packed at the bottom of the vase and slightly yellow. The flowers at the top burst from this foundation, the heads of blood red at the edge of the petals washing into an orange at the centre. One or two stray tulips hung out farther to the side than the rest, giving the display a naturalistic, busy look. She caught the perfume of the flowers, lifted by the sweep of the warm air around the room.

The food was crisp and clean. A salad with

chicken and a very light dressing. The bread was warm from the oven and various cheeses were laid out along with fruit. She drank another glass of wine. She felt the atmosphere relax, any earlier tension disappearing.

'Did you know your father's second wife?' she asked.

'After the divorce, the only times I spent with my father, until I was seventeen, were here at the house. I would see her then.'

'Did you get on with her?'

'She was always very kind. I think she was ashamed almost. That she had taken our father away from us. We did not really mind. It was an adventure, living between two parents. And then of course, she died.'

It came out sounding inevitable. Not cold towards his stepmother, but cynical and resigned.

'Father has never recovered,' he went on. 'They say things about him. That he is strange, that he does not like to go out, things like that. It has been hard for him.'

'Do you think he will marry again?'

Max shook his head. 'No.'

'And you?'

'I have no plans to. It is not likely.'

The maid brought a tray with some pastries on.

'Anne-Marie, will you set some candles in the pool please?'

She nodded and left.

'You have a pool?'

'Of course. Two in fact. There is one outside, off to the side of the house.' He pointed. 'But there is one indoors. Not as big. An overgrown bathtub, father calls it. I like to relax in it in the afternoon. You are welcome to if you wish.'

He looked away, unable to meet her eyes. She

wanted to ask him a question, but it seemed too personal. Instead, she drained the wine from her glass and said, as much to herself as to him, 'Why not?'

She was taken aback by the pool. She had, for some reason, been expecting something rather drab and municipal. This was a verdant paradise. The pool itself would have been no more than ten feet by fifteen – a big bath, as Max Ruga had quoted his father. The room was heavy with white marble and stone, right the way to the grand steps that led into the pool. Palms and other green plants were placed around the small room in pots. A tiny round table and two chairs nestled in one corner. There was the sound of running water. The pool was warm, she could tell from the humidity.

The windows were shuttered, obliterating almost all of the sunlight, and the room was lit by candlelight. Dozens of them. All of them small, low candles like night-lights, in small glass holders of varying colours. The candles flickered and danced, making shadows from the plants play against the walls, highlighting the greenery against the white marble. On the surface of the water there were floating candles of a frosted orange colour in large saucer-like holders. They gave off a scent like dewberry or geranium. Several water lilies lolled about the surface of the water.

By the side of the pool, in one large spectacular display, were calla lilies. The thick stems, wider at the bottom, tapered into the flowers – blooms that began as a bulge at the tip of the stalk, undulating roundly before blossoming into a single large petal that was turned back on itself. The whiteness of the petals, she saw as she moved closer, was ridged and grooved with veins that crinkled along the surface. From the hollow at the centre of the flower, the stamen protruded, rough and pointed. She inhaled the bouquet.

She turned to look at Max. He was removing his t-shirt. He threw it on to a chair. His torso had the faintest covering of dark hair, his skin more olive on his body than his face. He sat and pulled off his Chelsea boots, then removed his trousers and underwear. Unselfconsciously, he stood naked before her. She looked at him. He was an inch or so shorter than her, his build stocky, more noticeable now he was nude. His arms were solid and his legs muscled. His cock hung loosely between his legs, not showing any sign of stirring in her presence. As he walked off to the pool, she looked at his firm behind, the cheeks moving up and down with each step. He entered the pool carefully, moving between the lilies and candles. Slowly, his naked form was swallowed by the water as he sat down in the pool.

The wine had transported Andrea to one of her favourite places. She felt as though she weighed less and that the thoughts in her mind were able to arrange themselves perfectly, filtered through the gentle buzz of the alcohol. The humidity in the room was pleasant, the glimmer and glow of the candles comforting. The smell of the flowers and of the candles lifted her. She thought about Max naked in the pool, the warm water flowing all around him.

She removed her clothes quickly. The air in the room wafted on to her body. Her breasts fell free and they felt heavy, the tips hardening. In her stomach, her groin and her crotch, there was a tingle. It was anticipation and desire, her body sending her signals, relaying its urges to her consciousness.

The water was warm on her foot as she placed it on the first step. The steps were long and wide, enabling a leisurely descent into the water. The water lapped over the top of her foot and she took another step down. Max was watching her and she enjoyed the feeling of stepping slowly down the stairs, her supple body on display.

When the water was up above her knees, she descended a little more quickly, eager to get the water around her pussy. It touched her lips and she shivered. If flowed around the cheeks of her rear and up between the tops of her legs. It lapped at her pubic hair. She stayed standing in the same position, rocking her body gently back and forth, a small wave started to break against her crotch. It was slow and insistent, gentle enough to stimulate but not hard enough to release her. She was tempted to reach down for herself, but resisted.

Andrea bent her knees and sat down on the bottom step. Her breasts floated in the water and felt weightless. She splashed water carefully over them, brushing against her erect nipples. The water enveloped her and bathed her. It was warm and scented, the smell of geranium coming from its very surface rather than the many candles that floated about. The large, buoyant holders were clear thin glass and the light from them was bright orange.

She wondered if he would make the first move. She doubted it. She was not sure he even wanted to make a move at all. The question that had crossed her mind earlier returned. She looked at him and thought about asking him about women. As if he had read her mind and did not want to hear her questions, he dipped his head under the water. When it reappeared, he looked different, cleansed.

Momentarily, she moved into a squatting position as she rose from the bottom step. The cheeks of her rear were spread and the water felt cool inside. She stood and walked towards him, the water running off her as she did so, trickling down her breasts and on over her stomach. It dripped from her pubic hair which just skimmed the water line and felt moist and itchy.

He stood as she approached him. She noticed the way his cock had become long and loose in the heat of the water. It was dangling heavily between his legs. The candles floated around them and the light caught the rivulets of water on his torso and filled them with a glow. As she neared him, she could sense his tension, his anxiety and his desire to know.

In her hand, his cock had an impressive heft and weight. She squeezed at it and it pulsed back at her, expanding her grip on it. The skin on his shaft was soft and ruffled, the veins hiding beneath the sheath at that moment, but threatening to stand proud with some encouragement from Andrea. She cupped his balls in her fingers. Covered with a light smattering of hair, the sac was suspended freely. With her fingers, she played at his member, manipulating and moulding it, shaping it to size. It became firmer. She looked up at him.

'Do you want to touch me?' she said.

'Yes,' he replied hoarsely, nodding at the same time.

Andrea sat back on one of the higher steps, the water just covering her pussy, like the tide coming in on a beach. Through the water, the light refracted on her and she could see her pussy blurred by the water and illuminated by the glint of candles. She opened her legs and they were heavy in the water as it gushed around her. She placed her hands on the lips of her vagina and pulled herself open. The water found her like a flood, sluicing at her and tickling her clitoris, making it throb against the warm wave.

'Touch me,' she said to him.

Max reached his hand out and it submerged just under the surface of the water. The fingers of his right hand were all about her pussy in an instant, fevered and slightly clumsy. She reached and held his hand in hers. She guided it to her clitoris, moving his fingers so they were positioned around it. Still gripping him, she helped him make the correct rhythmic motions. She let this continue, the passion building. She grasped one of his fingers at its base and pushed it up inside her, gasping at the invasion that was propelled by the force of her own hand.

'Squeeze it lightly,' she said, when he had withdrawn the finger of his own accord and began concentrating on her clitoris.

Having shown him the way, she left him to gently manoeuvre his fingers over her. The feeling was like a key, a code in her that would be cracked. It was a code imprinted deep in her senses, decipherable only by a combination of each sense working together and pushing her in a single direction. She rested her elbows on the steps and listened to the sound of his hand moving about in the water, splashing like a fish.

Her orgasm came quickly and was rough with her, playing nerve-endings off against each other and pushing blood at a high pressure into her farthest reaches. She clamped her hand back on to his as she came, holding him closer to her and making him a part of her. It was a brief and potent orgasm, one that signalled a beginning rather than an end.

Shadows played around the walls of the pool room, enclaves of darkness formed by the intersection of candlelight. Her skin was warm and slippery from the lubricant effect of the water. She felt a languor, a laziness induced by the force of her orgasm. The water made a faint, rolling sound and any movement through it was amplified, sounding fluid and with an echo that betrayed the size of the room.

Andrea stood and touched his body. She held his arms and felt the muscle of his biceps and the well-formed triceps on his outer arm. She touched his chest, front and sides, the heat of his skin on her palms. She traced her fingers delicately on his forehead and then ran them through the dark, damp mop of black hair. She pulled him close to her and hugged him tightly, their damp bodies clinging to each other. It felt like a gesture of thanks from Andrea to him, for bringing her pleasure and a promise of more.

Still in an embrace, her chin resting on his shoulder, she arched her body slightly away and reached down for him. He was stiff, and she moved his rigid cock against her groin, feeling the straight and simple hardness of it on her soft skin. She played the tip into the fleece of her pubic hair. Gently, she pulled the foreskin back and forth and he let out a small cry against her ear as she did. She masturbated him more firmly and his hold on her tightened, his body moving back and forth. She stopped before he came, squeezing his cock tight and sealing him back up.

She planted a kiss under his jaw. She bristled

her hand through the hair on the back of his neck and pulled back to look at him. His eyes looked intense, the eyebrows set even heavier than earlier. Tentatively, he pouted and moved towards her. She received the nervous kiss and responded forcefully with one of her own. Taking hold of his hands she pulled him along with her as she walked backwards through the water and towards the side of the pool.

Sitting on the edge of the pool, she carried on kissing him carelessly, his mouth beginning to relax and move with hers. As he stood, so his cock was level with her pussy. She gripped it and eased the foreskin back, watching the glans ripple and tremor as she did so. She hoped his unsheathed cock would be able to find its way without too much guidance from her.

Now she lay right back on the side of the pool and looked at the ceiling, the marble against her back. She drew her legs up, holding them behind the knees, and felt wide open and ready.

The lower part of her body, the curve of her rear and her pussy, overhung the edge of the pool by just a fraction. The water lapped just a few inches below, but it could have been a drop of miles. She felt giddy, as though she were on the edge of a sheer precipice and about to jump into the void.

She heard a ripple, the sound of him moving closer to her. Reaching her hand down she parted herself a fraction. Her body was still covered by a film of the water and the air in the room was warm and drying her to a softness. Like the waves of the pool, she felt fluids stir in her, hot and deep. She wanted to wash over him with them.

The hardness of his cock was a shock to her as

it made its entrance. It was with a slow and careful movement that it infiltrated her. It opened her and she received it easily, her vagina expanding and its lubrication easing the path of his stern shaft.

When it was fully inside her, she felt no contact with his body other then where his cock was. By lying back on the side of the pool with her legs drawn up, she was able to present herself in a way that enabled him to penetrate her in a precise and deep way without seeing her or touching her. She wondered if she had not subconsciously adopted the position to allow him to fuck her without getting too close. She sensed that he may not have been comfortable with that. Certainly, even though he was now deep inside her, she did not feel his hand anywhere on her.

It was like being fucked by a cock alone. She lay on the side of the pool, listening to the sound of the water and to the small, involved grunts that Ruga's son made as he entered her with deep strokes. His cock was virtually parallel with her vagina and he was able to push in and out of her in a way that felt as though it went to her very centre.

A precise angle of entry, it soothed the aching of her pussy. His thrusts were long and slow, prolonging the pleasure for both of them. He was like a flower blossoming inside her each time he delved himself fully into her. The head of his cock pushed against the walls of her pussy and the top of his shaft grazed the underside of her clitoris.

She could not be precise as to how long it lasted. It felt like hours. The rigid cock slipped in and out of her sopping pussy and she held on to her orgasm for as long as she could, keeping it for herself for a while longer. She nurtured it inside herself, letting the images and feelings make different patterns in her mind. Various pleasures played before her and the feeling of him inside her drove them like an engine. When she was ready, the passion that had been pent up inside her would burst out and make itself known.

The full lips of her pussy were alive with the sensation of him moving against her and her clitoris tingled from his exertions. She pulled her legs tighter to herself, making every last centimetre of herself available to be ransacked by him.

His thrusting had become more of a deep lunge and it pushed her body backwards as he slapped into her. It was as though he were trying to wrench his come from himself and fire far inside her. He whispered under his breath and she heard his breathing become erratic. The cock that was tunnelling into her was about to pulsate and shoot inside her.

As he came, he shouted and growled. And for the first time, she felt him on her. He had leaned forward and was resting his hands on the side of the pool. His inner forearms were against her sides. She pulled her head to watch him orgasm. His eyes were shut and full lips a-tremor. His mouth was open and there was a look as much of surprise as ecstasy on his face. With each spurt, he squinted, his nose scrunching up and his teeth baring.

Inside her, the come was hot and thick. She felt it spurt within her and contracted around him as it did so, a spasm of her own building.

'Don't stop,' she called to him.

His cock spilled on into her; hot and slick it drove itself along her vagina and flooded her with semen. She came in a single, unbroken wave. It was as though she had stepped over the earlier, imagined precipice and was falling through the air. The sensation was powerful and incessant, not giving her a chance to think, just to feel. She arched her back and felt her spine lift and tense and then relax again. She sobbed and lifted herself, lunging at him this time as she finally felt the wave break. She compressed his cock inside of her, rippling around it as she felt him judder.

He had placed his hands on his head and was running them through his hair, the last of his orgasm still causing him to twitch and quiver.

When he had withdrawn from her, she sat up and looked at his cock, its hardness subsiding. She dropped her feet back into the water and then let her whole body slip into the warm blanket of geranium, her pussy welcoming the soothing caress of the water.

He came to her and squatted level with her. She put her arms around him and he rested his head on her shoulder. Smoothing his hair, she felt his breath against her cheek.

By the time she left, late in the evening, the candles in the pool had burnt down to nothing.

Chapter Twelve

FOR THE THIRD time that day, she listened to the soft burr of Philip's voice. Even though the message on his machine was in Italian and she could pick out only a few words, his voice and tone were familiar to her. She replaced the receiver and wondered where he was.

Andrea had been back from Nice for two days and had not been able to contact Philip. No one at Sandros knew where he was. She was getting anxious about Ruga. It was almost a week since Philip had told her about the re-launch of Onyx and she had gathered some limited information, but in the main Ruga was a trail of dead ends. She knew more about the shoes than she did about the man who designed them.

Several pairs of Onyx shoes were in her wardrobe at home, having been hastily purchased in Camden Market on Sunday. They were, in themselves, nothing spectacular – a sort of cross between a walking boot and a running shoe. What they had going for them was a cult status. She knew from experience that something did not need to be special to be sold, it just needed to be sold. In her mind, she had already formulated some ideas about how they would push the Onyx range, trading on the re-launch of a retro classic. There were endless possibilities to use some of the original campaign and to fuse it with new elements. All of that, of course, was dependent on her being in a position to convince Ruga that this was the approach to take.

It was never easy to go cold to the head of a corporation and it would be even harder given that Ruga did not act like the head of a corporation. He may have gone underground after his second wife died, but his busines still functioned – with or without him.

Once it was known that there would be a Ruga account, a scramble would follow from every agency to woo the man himself. DRA would certainly be among the suitors, but Andrea doubted she would be included in the courting ritual.

Tim had been gathering information for her, but had quickly reached the point where there was nothing more to research. Besides, Tim had come to her yesterday with a piece of information about DRA which was equally interesting if completely unrelated.

Gillian was fucking Martin.

When Tim had told her, it took a few minutes for the information to sink in. While he was enthusiastic about it, enjoying the gossip factor, Andrea had let it filter in and started to think about it. She could not imagine what anyone could possibly see in either of them and it was that which made her think they were made for each other. Andrea was not in the habit of regretting sleeping with someone, but in Martin's case she had made an exception.

Apart from a few heated phone calls, a couple

of strained encounters and a few days of awkwardness between them, Andrea thought that her and Martin's splitting up had worked out well enough. She did not expect him to become her new best friend. Now, she wondered if Martin was seeing Gillian as a way of retaliating. But that was not his style. Perhaps Gillian was doing it to get at her? Again, unlikely. Andrea did not figure in the situation as far as she could tell, but something about it troubled her. The union of Martin and Gillian was not a pleasant thought – physically or commercially. Instinctively, she felt there must be a way for her to make some capital from the situation, to fit it into the overall scheme of things. It would come to her, eventually, but for the moment it was hidden from her view, like the title of a book she could not remember or the name of a supporting actor. It would come to her.

Her phone rang the single trill indicating it was internal.

'Andrea King.'

'Hi, it's me.' It was Deanna.

'How are you?'

'I'm fine,' said Deanna. 'We should go for coffee. I've got something that you'll find interesting.'

'Let's go for cappuccino at Stefan's. Now?'

'See you in reception in five minutes.'

Stefan's was the sandwich bar around the corner from DRA. It did a good trade from all the local offices, but DRA was its biggest single source of income. People would drop by and pick up coffee ad pastries on their way into the office. Stefan's would even bring things around to the office if they were asked. One of the brothers who worked there had a security pass for DRA and could often be seen entering the building carrying a small box filled with Styrofoam cups. Andrea was always expecting to hear that Carl Anderson had bought Stefan's. For all they knew, he may even have owned it and employed the people in there as spies.

'Ladies,' beamed the older of the two brothers. 'Two cappuccinos, one bagel – plain – and a danish with apricot?' he continued, pleased with himself that he knew them and their habits so well.

'You could just eat it for us as well,' Deanna said to him.

They went and sat down. There were several people from DRA occupying tables, all engaged in some conspiracy or other. Nods and glances were exchanged. Andrea and Deanna sat in one of the window tables away from the main throng. The sun was shining through the window and it reminded Andrea of Rome and Nice.

The sandwich bar was small and the tables functional. Paper serviettes in black and chrome dispensers were on all the tables and the chairs were a seventies square design with wood frames painted red and basket seats. Stefan's was staffed by two brothers, their sister, and sundry first-generation Italians of varying relationships to the siblings. It was never fully clear who was in charge or quite what the long running argument in Italian was about, but the young blood seemed to have the upper hand.

'So, what's the big news?' asked Andrea when they were settled.

'They're bringing forward the last module of MCC.'

'When to?'

'Week after next. Wednesday. And they're moving it to the Crayford Hotel in London.'

Their coffee arrived. The older brother smiled and flirted with Deanna and they talked for a few moments about football. He played in a Sunday league and was still trying to convince Deanna to go and see him play. Andrea toyed at the frothy milk with her spoon, stirring the chocolate into the surface of the liquid. She broke a small piece of her bagel and chewed on it whilst the older brother continued his pitch.

When he left them, Andrea raised her eyes.

'I think he's nice,' said Deanna, defending herself against Andrea's dismissive expression.

'Christ, footballer's legs. No thanks. Anyway, MCC3.'

'Yes. It's in London, a week on Wednesday. But that's not the biggest news. Anderson is going to attend. He's scheduled to be there all morning.'

'He won't make an announcement there though,' said Andrea, moving her cup about on the saucer. 'Not all the principals will be there.'

'No, I don't think he will. How can he have selected anybody yet? There's been no interviews or anything,' said Deanna.

'It's like he announced it and then forgot about it. Everyone else is scrabbling about, wondering what they can do to impress him and he is just as serene as ever. It's very clever. What he's done is removed any conventional criteria for selecting someone. At the end of the day, it comes down to his whim. And, to be honest, he might as well draw this one out of a hat.'

They sat in silence for a moment, drinking coffee and picking at their respective plates. Andrea continued.

'Why would Anderson come to the last module of MCC3? Did they move it forward just so he could attend?'

148

'That's what I heard. He's probably just got a fit in his head about wanting to do some hands-on. It's not major information, but I thought you'd like to know. Maybe you'll get a chance to impress him there. As far as I know, it's not going to be announced that Anderson will be there, just that the module's been moved forward.'

'I appreciate it,' said Andrea. 'I'll make sure I've done all the necessary prep for it. You know what it's like usually – seat-of-the-pants job.'

'How's Tim?'

'Talking of seat of the pants, you mean?'

Deanna sniggered. 'In a manner of asking.'

'He's a horny little bastard, since you ask.'

'Well, grab him before the decline sets in. He's in his prime.'

'I don't think I've got him quite to his prime – yet.'

'But is he any good, And?'

'Getting better,' she said, adopting her stage prime voice at which they both cackled. 'Actually, he told me something interesting yesterday, about Martin and Gillian.'

'I know, I'd heard that,' said Deanna, shuddering. 'It's an awful thought.'

'What's she up to? Does she really think Martin can help her? He's as bad as her. He'll help himself first, just like the rest of us.'

'She's pissing everyone off, And. She lauds it around our area like she owns the fucking place. Almost everyone I can think of has some gripe or grudge.'

'I think that's why she's there,' sighed Andrea, breaking another piece of bagel. 'Her work is never better than average, but she goes round the whole time like a bitch on wheels.'

'Bitch on roller skates, actually. Her secretary

told me that she keeps track of Gillian's menstrual cycle on her year planner so she knows when to avoid her. Do you think she'll get this job?'

'Not if I have anything to do with it. It must be on her mind, Deanna. Why else would she come over from Goldman Miller to here? She was more high powered over there. This wasn't even a sideways move.'

'Terry at Goldman's was saying she jumped before the push came. Maybe it was all she could get.'

'I'd like to know. I need to get back, Deanna. I imagine you'll have no argument with lingering on your own for a moment longer and paying big brother,' Andrea said, getting to her feet.

The row started simply.

Earlier in the week, before she left for Nice, Andrea was asked to produce a forecast. It was a simple and partly pointless exercise in which she tried to guess the amount of revenue she would bring in from her major accounts over DRA's coming year. It was something that Carl Anderson asked for at varying points through the year and it filtered down through the structure, from people like Martin and Carol, and then on to people like Andrea, account managers and handlers.

It was a process of trying to make steak out of mincemeat as the figures gradually Chinese-whispered their way back up to the top. Somewhere in the midst of all this, Carl Anderson was able to divine some sense of how well his agency would do in the coming year. This time around, Martin had requested a quality forecast. Andrea wondered if this was simply an attempt to seem thorough for Anderson's benefit or if Anderson himself had requested it, possibly because he was seriously thinking of selling DRA or perhaps floating it on the stock market. She would have to pump Philip for more information. She was sure he knew more than he had told her about DRA.

With all of these considerations, Andrea had thought a little longer than usual about the forecast before giving it to her assistant, Julie, who would collate the information and put it into the standard format.

After she arrived back from her coffee at Stefan's, she happened to be at the photocopier at the same time as Julie, who was taking copies of the forecast. Julie asked her if she wanted a copy and Andrea had said yes. While she waited for Julie to finish, Andrea stood and glanced over the forecast, something she would not normally take the time to do.

'Julie, there's a mistake here.'

Julie looked up from the copier and came to look at the sheet of paper with Andrea, a worried look on her face.

'Where?' she said.

'This figure for Lazzo, under the new business section. I put one and a quarter million on the forecast, not half a million.' She pointed her finger at the space on the page.

Julie looked and concentrated on the page.

'Oh, that,' she said, recognition coming over her face. 'Gillian told me to change it.'

'I'm sorry?'

'Gillian. She said the forecast figure should be half a million. I was going to put a note on your copy.'

Julie's words were already distant as Andrea strode towards her office and slammed the door shut.

Andrea knew that when she was angry, it was best to give herself a breather. Not to calm down, but to formulate the best response she could. She was more spiteful when she was calm than when she was overheated.

Gillian Kay had changed Andrea's figures. The forecast was Andrea's and Andrea's alone. Gillian had her own accounts and did her own forecast reports for them. There was no overlap between the two of them and she had no place to make any input whatsoever into Andrea's accounts unless requested by Andrea. Or someone else? Martin? What would the point be of modifying her figure downwards? If Andrea wanted to shaft someone, she would increase their forecast. All she could think of was that Gillian was an interfering bitch.

Andrea picked up the receiver and called Martin's number. His assistant said he was out at a meeting and wouldn't be back until late afternoon. She called Gillian Kay's number. Her secretary answered.

'Kelly, put me through to Gillian.'

'She's not answering calls now, Andrea,' came back the happy Australian voice.

'Is she in her office?'

'Yes, but she's not . . .'

'Put me through, Kelly, now. She'll talk to me.'

She waited and listened to the silence of the phone system as she was put on hold.

'Andrea,' said Gillian enthusiastically. 'Where's the fire?'

'Why did you change the Lazzo number?'

'I meant to mention that to you.'

'Why did you change the Lazzo number?' she repeated, already hearing Gillian's tone falter.

'I thought it looked a little high, that was all.'

'How did you come to see my forecast, Gill?'

'When I was at Goldman, I tried to work that account. Nothing ever came of it. I thought it would be better . . .'

'Perhaps that's why you're no longer at Goldman. How did you see my forecast, Gill?'

'One and a quarter was a bit high,' Gillian spluttered, not answering the question and trying to add a friendly chuckle to the end of the sentence.

'Did Martin show it to you?'

'Martin?'

'Yes, you know. Tall, dark hair, average-sized cock. Martin. Did he show it to you?'

'Andrea, there's really no need to take that tone. I thought it would be doing you a favour.'

'Can I give you some advice on how to do yourself a favour? Do not ever do anything like that again. If you do, I'll make sure you're out of here. Do you understand me?'

'Don't overestimate yourself, Andrea, and don't overstep the mark with me.'

'Gill, live in the real world. I'm going to hang this phone up now. Just think on what I said. I know DRA better than just about anyone. It's not worth tangling with me. Ask around.'

Whatever Gillian said next, Andrea did not hear. All she heard was the slam of the phone as she banged it down forcefully into the cradle.

Since Gillian had arrived at DRA, Andrea had not let her anger spill over. It was never wise to do so until you understood where someone was located in the agency, officially and unofficially. Now, she had vented some fury and it felt good. She doubted it would have any repercussions. She would get the forecast figure changed back and leave it at that for the moment.

Her phone rang a minute or two later. She

switched it on to her other line and called Julie on her main one, telling her she was not taking calls. Julie buzzed back almost immediatley.

'Julie, no calls,' she snapped into the phone.

'There's a Max Ruga to see you, in reception,' said Julie.

Chapter Thirteen

ANDREA LOOKED AROUND in reception and then asked John the security guard where Max Ruga was.

Her heart had begun pounding with excitement as she rode down in the elevator, partly from the prospect of meeting Ruga and partly in fear that somebody would spot him and recognise him, however unlikely that was.

'Over there,' said John, in his usual offhand manner, pointing to the sofa as though it should have been obvious.

A woman in her mid-twenties sat on the deep, soft brown leather sofa. She wore blue jeans and a blue denim jacket. Her white blouse was unbuttoned to the third button down, revealing cleavage. The sleeves of the denim jacket were turned back two or three times and she wore a heavy gold Rolex Oyster watch. The ensemble was topped off by a black Nike baseball hat and bottomed out by a pair of pointed cowboy boots with a silver rim around the outside edge of the toecap.

'Andrea?' the woman questioned, rising from the sofa and holding out her hand. Her tone and demeanour were cool and calm.

'My brother told me what you looked like. I'm Maxine Ruga.'

She paused.

'Max for short.'

There was evident satisfaction in her expression at the fact that Andrea had obviously been expecting her father.

Her nails were long and manicured, painted a curdling shade of red. Long chestnut brown hair turned up at its ends, just shy of her shoulders. Her face was fresh with clear and clean-looking tanned skin that made it hard for Andrea to imagine that the olive-skinned Max and she were indeed brother and sister. The heavy-set eyebrows were the giveaway.

'What can I do for you?' Andrea asked, wondering how much more than just what she looked like her brother had told her of their encounter in Nice two days earlier.

'I am here in London on business for my father. Max thought you were interested in speaking to Father about something connected with business. I may be able to help you. And, I was curious to meet you.' The final sentence sounded like a concession.

'Curious?'

'Yes. There are few, very few, women who get my brother animated. You appear to be one such woman.'

This time, she sounded superior, jealous almost.

'No offence, but I would prefer to talk directly with your father,' Andrea said.

'I may be as close as you will get. Max said you were evasive about your reasons for seeing father. I expect it was obvious to you that my brother is

156

not really involved in the family's business affairs.'

Would this be as close as she would get, Andrea asked herself. She never believed in going through levels to reach the person she really needed to talk to. But this was not like that. This would be like getting close to Ruga in a different way. She needed time to consider it. More time than she had standing in the reception of DRA.

'Perhaps we could talk over lunch?' Andrea suggested.

'I have a lunch appointment. Later on this afternoon?'

'I'm in meetings all afternoon.'

Maxine scrunched her face, 'I'm booked all day. Could we have dinner, perhaps?'

Andrea thought. 'Yes. Where?'

'London is more your town than mine,' Max smiled. 'I am only half-English.' The distance and loftiness had disappeared.

'How would pizza, Californian-style, sound?'

'I think it would sound like blasphemy.' Again a smile.

'Trust me,' said Andrea, taking one of her business cards from a pocket on the inside of her jacket. 'This is my home address,' she said, turning the card over. 'I make a very good pizza.'

'Are you sure it will not be too much trouble?'

'Definitely not. Eight-thirty?'

'It is more likely to be nine.'

'No problem. My number's on the card, so call me if you run into any difficulty.

Andrea wanted to be careful to take the time to explore the opportunity with Maxine. Having her over to dinner, moving her on to her own territory, was risky and a little familiar, but

Andrea believed that beneath the cool façade there was a person she could relate to. Nothing about the Rugas was conventional, so she decided that the less conventional her approach, the better. A curiosity emanated from Maxine, a desire about what Andrea wanted and what she meant to her brother. A curiousness that was not unlike her brother's. She hoped to be able to use all of this. If she seemed willing to listen and she was genuinely important in her father's business, she would ask her questions about the re-launch of Onyx.

She went and spoke to Tim.

'Guess who was just in reception?' she said quietly, looking around her as she did so.

Tim looked up at her and removed his round reading spectacles. His face wore an expression that said 'Who?'

'Ruga's daughter, Maxine.'

'Here?'

'Yes, here. She turned up in reception and announced herself as Max Ruga. I was there before the receiver was down. Her brother told her who I worked for. I think she may be useful, but I can't tell yet.'

'Is she still here?'

'No. I'm seeing her later. She's coming over to my place around nine. I'm making dinner.'

He looked at her. 'And you want me to not really be there, right?'

She looked at him. His expression was clear and youthful and yet so insightful. Eager to please as ever, like the first time in the sick room and on numerous occasions since then. She felt an urge to reach out and touch him but resisted it.

'I need to get her alone,' was all she said.

'I was going to go home tonight anyway,' he said unconvincingly.

'Come over later. I'd like that,' she said. She handed him the spare keys to her flat.

He looked at them resting on his palm and said, 'Around midnight?' then closed his hand over them.

The bases of the two pizzas had risen to exactly the required degree and she chopped the last of the spinach she was going to use for the topping, along with sun-dried tomatoes, mange tout, bell peppers, a little avocado and some baby corn. She had made a gentle salsa sauce and this she would smear thinly over the base. The salad was already made and in the fridge chilling, along with some bottles of Chardonnay. She picked the open bottle out of the cooler and poured herself a glass of wine. She went to finish setting the table.

It was eight-fifteen. She sat on her large sofa and sipped from the glass, feeling the relaxing surge from her ankles all the way up to her shoulders. Music played quietly in the background and the room lighting was subdued, lamps pointing at various discreet angles. Knots in her body untied themselves and tense muscles slackened. The table was laid. A crisp pink cotton cloth and white napkins. She had not gone wildly overboard and the table looked simple and inviting.

Tim would not be there until at least midnight. There would be enough time, she thought. Spending the amount of time she did in restaurants and out with clients, travelling and working long hours, she rarely entertained at home. It was a shame because she enjoyed it. She let the music carry her off and her mind went into neutral.

When the doorbell rang, it startled her. She

checked her watch. It was nine-twenty. Where had the time gone?

Maxine had changed. A lustrous camel hair coat blanketed her curvaceous body and the denim was replaced by a dress not quite skimpy enough to be a cocktail dress or light enough to be a summer dress, but somewhere between the two.

'You found it?' Andrea said, standing in the doorway.

'The taxi driver found it. Sorry I am late. I would have been even later but you are so close to the centre of town. I would have called you but my telephone does not work here. What a wonderful location.'

'It's an indulgence of mine,' Andrea said, showing her in and closing the door behind her.

After Andrea had pointed a few things out in a relatively formal manner, they sat on the sofa. Andrea poured wine for Maxine and refilled her own glass. For nearly twenty minutes they exchanged pleasantries that revolved around London, the weather, travel and Andrea's living-room. Andrea went to the kitchen to put the pizzas in the oven, declining Maxine's offer of help. When she returned from the kitchen, the look on Maxine's face had altered and become more serious and business-like.

'Tell me about DRA,' she said.

'We are the largest privately held advertising agency in the country. One of the five largest in Europe. As you can imagine, we are a combination of client-side account executives and more inwardly-facing creative and technical people. We have some major accounts for whom we set the direction, the tone and the look. We also do one-off campaigns for clients. We can get involved in any sort of media activity through print to television and radio, above and below the line. If we can't do it ourselves, we know people who can. There are designers, copywriters and so on. We are able to provide a complete range of services to help clients bring products to market, maintain the market, increase the market.' She ended on Carl Anderson's favourite line about market share.

'Do you think any of that would be of use to Max Ruga?' Maxine asked. 'Does he impress you as the sort of man who would want publicity?'

'I'm liable, almost duty-bound, to say everyone does at some time or other. I suppose the question is, is that time now? Perhaps it's a question I can ask you?'

If she did know the answer to the question, she was not at that moment supplying it. Instead, she ran a finger around the rim of her wine glass and peered at its contents. The silence hung heavy and Andrea felt a door close on the subject. She stood, saying she needed to check on the oven.

'The house in Nice is wonderful,' said Andrea, cutting a small piece of pizza.

'We grew up with it, partly, and do not appreciate it. As an outsider you see it differently, I am sure. Did you spend long there?'

'Your brother and I had lunch. It was a beautiful day.'

'This pizza is very good, really,' said Maxine.

'Not too blasphemous, I hope? A profane pizza.'

'Definitely not,' Maxine laughed.

The evening moved along and they chatted. It was a warm and pleasant feeling. Maxine had classic manners and enjoyed company. She was easy to talk with and carried herself gracefully. She looked after several of her father's subsidiary companies and had studied in the States, a Stanford MBA. She was bright and charming. It was eleven-fifteen when they were on the sofa drinking coffee and nibbling on amaretti biscuits.

'Andrea,' she said, 'why don't you tell me what this is about? I will pretend I don't know and you can surprise me.'

Andrea grinned at her.

'I hear, through a source I will not name, that the Onyx range may be re-launched. If that's true, it's big news and big business. I want a piece of it. Somebody will need to co-ordinate the campaign. Am I surprising you so far?'

Maxine did not speak.

'With the right approach, we could turn Onyx from a cult classic into a world-beater. It sounds like a cliché, but it's true. I think we should actively involve your father in the campaign, use him as a model.'

'Now you are surprising me,' said Maxine. 'Father, a model.' She giggled.

'It's true though, isn't it? About the re-launch?'

Maxine looked at her and did not speak. Instead, she extended her hand and rested it very carefully on Andrea's. Andrea did not move or say anything. Silence amplified itself in the room. There was a complete and total stillness to the air, the room, to time itself. Whilst Andrea remained seated, Maxine knelt up on the sofa to her and kissed her on the mouth.

The kiss came from nowhere. It surprised Andrea. It shocked her. And yet, it felt like it was the right thing to happen. The touch of their lips was soft and gentle. It started with their lips, feeling their way tentatively. Then the motion

162

spread to the whole mouth and on to their jaws. Soon they were writhing together, heads turning and pushing at each other. Their bodies too had picked up on the motion. They had gone from a stillness to the first rumblings of a storm. Andrea opened her mouth wide and let Maxine in.

She felt Maxine's hand exploring the front of her dress. It ran over her breasts in a considered and lingering motion, the weight of her palm lifting her and weighing her in her hand. Maxine knelt up and sat astride Andrea, gyrating her rear into Andrea's lap. Their kissing had become a nipping action as though they were trying to take bites out of each other.

Maxine slipped back off Andrea's lap until she was kneeling on the floor in front of her. She brushed the backs of Andrea's stockinged calves and Andrea felt the static charge of desire send a tingle all the way up to the tops of her legs, where it nested in between them and buzzed. She felt Maxine's hands expertly undo her stockings and in seconds they were off, in a single deft whisk. Wasting no time, Maxine reached under Andrea's dress and removed her knickers. As they came away from her, Andrea was aware of the dampness between her legs and of the fabric that had just been removed. Her knickers looked forlorn in Maxine's grasp.

The red-nailed hand disappeared again up Andrea's skirt. She sat and watched, wide-eyed, seeing the hand move under her dress, the outline of it as it advanced towards her. She backed away slightly but opened her legs a touch wider. Andrea was breathing hard, waiting.

The finger found her wet pussy. It traced along her lips which felt heavy and engorged with blood. Juices lay just beyond the folds of skin and

Andrea could feel them ready to spill from her. The finger tickled and teased at her lips, the moisture from within gradually seeping through. Carefully, it explored the crease of skin and eventually it came across her clitoris. Maxine scooped at it with her finger, awakening it and stirring it, like an ember in a fire.

The main sound in the room was of Maxine's hand brushing at the material of Andrea's dress as she worked away at her clitoris. Andrea was wide-eyed and she stared down at her crotch as though she could see the orgasm that was about to happen.

As she came, she fixed her eyes on Maxine. She cried out and pushed herself down on to the seat, shoving her back stiffly against it. She rocked back and forth, air escaping her mouth through only the smallest of spaces. Her drenched pussy shrank around Maxine's finger and held on to it. She felt herself beating around it like a heart and the juices flowed from her.

When it had subsided, she took Maxine's hand, the one that had just brought her so much pleasure, and led her upstairs to the bedroom.

They removed each other's clothes. Andrea unzipped Maxine's dress and it dropped to the floor. She wore no bra. With her back still to her, Maxine knelt and removed her tights and underwear, displaying the full roundness of her behind. With equally adroit movements from Maxine, Andrea's dress was removed, as were her bra and suspender belt.

For a few moments they stood and looked at each other. Maxine moved closer to Andrea and they kissed again but more passionately and intimately than they had downstairs. Andrea smoothed her hands over Maxine's firm body.

The breasts were heavy and the nipples large. She dipped her head and bit at them, Maxine's hands running through her hair as she did so. Now she stood upright and pulled herself close to Maxine, feeling the contact of their pussies.

Andrea put her arms around Maxine, one of them running across her back. She felt the warmth of her skin, the spine protruding and the rounded bump of her shoulder blades. She stroked Maxine's buttocks and ran a finger down beneath them, feeling the back of Maxine's pussy. When her finger withdrew, it was wet.

Maxine lay on the bed and, next to her, Andrea brushed her forehead and planted a kiss on it. She felt lust deep inside herself. Moving herself into a kneeling position she put her head down into Maxine's crotch. She looked closely at her pussy. The pubic bone was proud and muscular, and her pubic hair was neatly waxed into a long rectangle. The lips of her pussy hung low and splayed themselves out. Following the grooves of skin inwards from the ends of the lips, Andrea saw the thin line where they started. The entrance to her.

Andrea pressed her mouth against the lips of Maxine's pussy. She heard her sigh and purr as she did so. She licked along the opening, feeling the warmth and tasting the faint musk of her vagina. She pressed more insistently and her tongue found its way through the lips. She pushed it towards the top of the slit and found Maxine's small and firm clitoris. She flicked at it with her tongue, feeling the heat and the fluidity of Maxine's pussy. She forced on into her, feeling the strain at the base of the tongue. Putting her fingers to Maxine's pussy lips, she eased them open and this gave her full access to Maxine's clitoris. The small bud was full and Maxine

165

moved around against the bed covers, as though trying to scratch an itch.

With her face pressed determinedly against Maxine's pussy, Andrea explored this woman. It was a body like her own. In so many ways it was incredibly familiar to her. In this way it was completely alien. And that made it even better. She wanted Maxine to come while she had her face in her, her tongue exploring her hole and working at her clitoris. Between her own legs she felt the desire building again.

Through the hungry sounds of her own mouth, she heard Maxine cry out and moan in Italian. Andrea's face was pulled further in Maxine's groin by her hand on the back of her head. Maxine's pussy was awash with her hot viscous juices and Andrea lapped at them, tasting them and immersing herself in them.

She felt Maxine's muscles stiffen and could sense the change in her clitoris. She was amazed to be in the depths of a woman while she came. She had never thought before what the sensation would be like. To see a pussy as it orgasmed, feel its spasms and tongue it as it convulsed. All the while Maxine was spending herself, Andrea kept the rhythm going, riding the pattern of Maxine's movements.

They held each other, small and quiet words passing between them.

They dozed.

'Oh, Max,' Andrea gasped as she awoke with a tongue on her pussy.

She reached down to hold Maxine's head and guide it. Instead of the long and soft hair of Maxine Ruga, her hands fell upon a short-cropped head.

It was Tim.

Startled, she opened her eyes wide and sat up on her elbows. Tim was naked and kneeling on the bed, his head buried between her legs. She looked to her side. Maxine lay asleep. She looked back at Tim, his head bobbing and moving in her, his tongue flicking around her pussy lips and coaxing her clitoris.

Maxine stirred and Andrea watched her face as she came awake. While she had been sleeping, she looked much more like her brother. Her face had taken on an intensity and seriousness, much like the expression her brother seemed always to be wearing. She looked disoriented when she opened her eyes, as though she were having trouble remembering where she was. Her eyes widened when she saw the two of them next to her.

Andrea reached a hand out for Maxine and she came to her. They kissed slowly and deliberately, their lips still numbed from their earlier exertions. Tim stopped what he was doing and sat on the bed, looking at them. Andrea looked at Tim's cock, which was half erect and quickly on its way to full size. She was about to reach for it when Maxine beat her to it.

Maxine closed her hand around Tim's shaft. Its swollen tip protruded through the top, where her thumb and index finger were curled into a circle. Tim had removed his face from Andrea and now knelt up on the bed. Using her hand as a sheath, Maxine brought the foreskin backwards and forwards, Tim's balls swinging as she did so. Maxine had a look of concentration on her face as she masturbated Tim. The head of his cock gleamed with the early signs of his come.

While the two of them knelt up on the bed, Maxine's hand moving quickly back and forth,

Andrea positioned herself so that her tongue could flick at the head of Tim's cock as it appeared in front of her face. Maxine moved her hand down the shaft a little way and stopped. His cock stood out and Andrea played at its tip with her lips, not taking it in her mouth but giving it the smallest of pleasures she could imagine.

Maxine released Tim's cock and turned around on the bed, going down onto all fours. She reached a hand under herself and used her fingers to push apart her buttocks. Pulled wide between her two fingers was the dark rose of her anus, quivering and trembling. It tensed and relaxed several times.

Tim looked at Andrea and raised his eyes. She looked back at him and made a shrugging motion. Andrea looked at Tim's cock and saw that it was fully erect. He certainly wanted to. She reached over and handed him a jar of cream from the side table.

As he applied the cream, first around the outside of her hole, Maxine was silent. When he began to explore her with his index finger, she lifted her shoulders and shook her head as though she were limbering up for exercises. The first joint of Tim's index finger was inside Maxine's rear and she wriggled herself about on it. Andrea watched as the whole of the finger entered Maxine. Tim pulled it back and then pushed it in again. He did this numerous times using deep and rhythmic strokes. He pulled out and layered more cream on to his index finger and also on to his middle finger. Carefully, he began to work two fingers in her.

When she was fully greased up and flexible, Tim leaned back on his hunches and slicked grease all over his cock. It shone in the light of the room, the veins standing out on the glistening shaft. He moved his hand over himself a number of times and Andrea watched his cock fill to the brim as he did so. He positioned himself behind Maxine.

Tim pushed the head of his cock into the opening of her anus. Maxine cried out and squinted her eyes shut. Andrea looked at Tim's face, the concentration on it. She saw his expression change and she knew that he had entered her. She looked at Maxine and her face too had changed. It was no longer an expression of pain, but one of ecstasy. Andrea watched as the shaft of Tim's cock disappeared between Maxine's buttocks. His balls hung from the base of his shaft and she watched them rest against the underside of Maxine's rear, near her pussy.

Andrea remained kneeling beside them, enjoying the view of Maxine kneeling wide on the bed, her shoulders low and buttocks high while Tim was kneeling behind her, his groin firmly against her rear and his cock buried deep inside her. He held the globes of her rear and began to fuck it.

The sound of Tim banging into Maxine was enough to make Andrea reach down and begin to work at her own pussy. As his hips thrashed there was a sound of skin on skin. It was a heavy sound, almost a thump as hipbones met rear end. The bed was moving from Tim's exertions and Maxine was rocked forward into it. She cried out and made encouraging noises to Tim.

It was fascinating to Andrea to watch the way Tim's cock entered and exited Maxine's anus. As he withdrew, so her muscles came back slightly, moving in concert with him. As he pushed back, they were not as amenable and Andrea saw the look on both their faces to indicate this. Tim's strokes were long and deep. She saw the familiar look on his face, the one he made when he was forcing blood deliberately into his cock so it would pulse and grow wider. As he did, Maxine gasped.

Maxine bucked and writhed herself in time with Tim, using her lower back to move her rear in the best way possible. Andrea watched the way the buttocks swelled and enlarged with her movements. Tim gripped her just above the hips and his thrusts became shorter and more agitated. He growled and snarled, the sweat building on his brow in a sheen. His powerful chest muscles rippled and his arms were tense, his grip on Maxine causing the muscles to flex. Maxine lay with the side of her head down on the bed and her hair flowed out against the covers. She nodded and shook her head, eyes shut and in a world of her own.

Andrea watched the whole scene with fascination. She enjoyed watching Tim with his lithe young body and strong cock as he fucked Maxine Ruga. It made Andrea feel dirty. She was enjoying being a spectator in their sex and she was looking forward to seeing both of them come. She wanted to watch their movements, to gauge the strength of their passions from the looks on their faces. And while all this was happening, she wanted to have an orgasm of her own.

She did not have to wait long.

Maxine raised herself up on her hands and let out a cry. She orgasmed with a force and volume level that filled the room. It was a loud moan that had been preceded by a series of short sobs. She ground herself back on to Tim's cock and shook her head furiously from side to side.

Tim let out a cry of his own and Andrea looked

at him. His mouth was slightly open and his eyes fluttered. He grimaced and Andrea watched the sweet contortion of the intense orgasm he was having. She thought about the hotness of his come, the way it would be flowing from his cock, the short sharp jets of it injecting Maxine's rear.

She could contain herself no longer. She employed one hand on herself, as she had been for the past several minutes, and with the other she reached and found where Tim was joined to Maxine. She felt the grease around the opening of Maxine's splayed anus. It was smeared along the top of Tim's cock as it came out of Maxine. She tried to push her finger in where Tim's cock was so deeply planting itself and as she did so she felt Maxine tremble.

Andrea snorted as she came. She finger-fucked herself with one hand and Maxine with the other. Tim had withdrawn his cock and Andrea had let her finger take its place. The passage was warm and loose where it had been invaded. She cried, resting part of her hand on Maxine's buttocks for support. She opened her eyes and looked at her fingers, the ones in herself and the ones in Maxine Ruga. The orgasm pumped her upwards, taking her gravity from her and rendering her vision pure white.

She fell down on to the bed, exhausted. Hands were over her rear and between her legs, whose she had no way of knowing. It was going to be a long night.

Chapter Fourteen

IT WAS, IN all likelihood, the nicest-looking collection of men she had seen in one place in a long time. Since her last visit to a place like this, she thought. Music was playing just louder than the sound of the average person's voice and she observed people talking loudly to each other in order to be heard.

The Brink was one of Soho's newer bars. A gay bar, but one where a whole mix of people went, especially at lunch-times. She knew two men who had thought of buying the original building and converting it into a multi-level bar. It had never happened. Someone else must have had the same idea and The Brink was born. She made her way upstairs to the eating area, where the tables were the same as downstairs but adorned with gingham cloths, laid for lunch. Philip was at one of the back tables with someone else.

'Angel,' he said, standing to kiss her.

His companion was in his mid- to late-twenties and stood awkwardly, as though he would not normally have been brought to his feet by the presence of a woman. He was pretty. His black hair was short and gelled close to his head, as though it were afraid to wander too far from it. He wore a tight white t-shirt that was ribbed longways.

'This is Callum,' said Philip, nodding towards the man who shook her hand, a small slightly impish smile on his face. They sat.

'How long have you been here?' she asked Philip.

'Only fifteen or so minutes.'

'No, in London I mean. I tried to call you after I got back. Then for four days after that. Even late last night. You're getting harder and harder to find.'

'I arrived last night. I called you first chance I had. Do you like this venue?' He looked around expansively, trailing an outstretched arm across the panorama.

'I've been here a few times. One of the designers, Jake, likes to come here at lunch-times. My friend Jerome brought me here one evening – I found it a bit, I don't know, arid?'

Philip laughed at her.

'Are you staying for long, in London?' she asked him.

'A flying visit as usual. A few pieces of business to conduct. Some information that will be useful for you.'

Andrea looked at Callum and did not know how much she should say in front of him. She stared at him for a moment and then looked back at Philip.

'Callum,' said Philip, picking up on Andrea's look, 'I need to talk to Andrea about business. I'll see you at the bar downstairs in a little while.' Philip reached out and held Callum's hand and Andrea watched as he squeezed it and looked into the man's eyes.

'Very nice,' she said, after Callum left and was making his way downstairs.

'Thank you. I hear a rumour about DRA. Is it true?'

'Depends on the rumour. What have you heard?'

'Anderson may be thinking of giving it all up. He's had enough. Wants to spend more time playing tennis and kicking people while wearing pyjamas.'

'We hear those ones all the time,' she said. 'You know he's looking to hire a Creative Director, in-house? There were some anonymous pieces in the trade press this week, gossip column stuff.'

'That one I had heard, yes. From Martin in fact. I believe he thought I may be able to do something for him.'

'And could you?'

'Angel, of course not. If I could do those sort of things, who do you think would be sitting in the chair right now?'

He rubbed the side of his head with one of his powerful hands.

She laughed. 'I can't work you out, Philip. I really can't.'

'What news of Nice?' he asked her.

'Strange,' she said. She proceeded to give him an account of her experience with Ruga's son. The story came out relatively coherently now she had spent some time thinking about it. He listened to her and nodded, smiling and occasionally gasping. She spared him no details.

'So you could say I deflowered him amongst the flowers,' she finished. She took a sip from the fizzy mineral water that had arrived somewhere in her recounting the story.

'But Ruga was not there?' Philip sighed, as

though exasperated, and rubbed his chin.

'No. And then the day before yesterday, the strangest thing of all happened. I got a call from the front desk and they told me Max Ruga was downstairs.'

Philip raised his eyebrows and sat back in his chair.

Andrea continued. 'It was his daughter, Maxine. I managed to find out from her that her father will be in London next week sometime.'

She decided to omit for the moment the details about Maxine, Tim and herself.

'You are getting ahead of the game, Angel. You will soon know more about this than I. Do you know how to get to him?'

She shook her head. 'No. I was literally thinking of camping out at the airport until he turns up. Maxine said she would call me later today with details of his itinerary.'

'You are not completely ahead of me, then. I can still be of some use to you. He's coming over to look at some paintings,' Philip said. 'They are in a private gallery. It's one of the few things that will bring him out. I hear that he is looking to buy some. Rothkos. Those dark colour field paintings. Intense dark squares on dark backgrounds.' He gave a pretend shudder.

'How do you know all this, Philip?'

'I know the man who had the collection. It was I who set up the viewing.'

'Couldn't you just schedule a meeting for Ruga and me while he's here?'

'It is not that simple. He is a complex, no, difficult man. I do not deal directly with him. The art thing happened purely by chance. I went through his son to set it up.'

'You know the son?'

175

He did not say anything. She looked at him, and the realisation dawned on her. She said nothing. She simply looked at Philip in silent acknowledgement.

'The gallery,' she said, leaning forward, 'is private. I have ensured that you will have sole access to it and to Ruga for the time he is there. He will expect you, but it is up to you to give him something he doesn't quite expect. I have every faith in you. You will need to give a very special pitch. The most important one ever. You will have only one chance to get it right. It is almost like a diamond robbery.'

For the next twenty minutes, Philip went through the details of how she must approach Ruga. Several times he explained what she would need to do. He spelled it out clearly.

'Philip, are you sure about this?' she asked him when he had finished.

'Trust me, Angel. This information is from the closest source.'

He reached down and fetched something from his bag and placed it on the table.

It was a box. A long rectangular box covered in a black animal skin of some kind that had a very close grain. Even though she knew, from the preceding twenty minutes of conversation, what would be in the box, it still surprised her. She gently undid the catch and lifted the lid. She looked and then carefully closed it.

'This is the real thing?' she asked him.

'The most real,' he smiled. 'An original. I heard that it may have been made by Michelangelo.' He gave a laugh.

Andrea tapped her mouth with her fingers for several moments.

'If it's the only way,' she said, taking the box

and putting it into her lap.

'The important thing,' he told her, 'is to get it right. To be thorough and accurate. To time it. If you need to practise, I am sure Callum would be more than willing to help you. I can talk to him, if you like?'

'No, that's okay,' she said to him.

'Whose is it?' said Tim, turning it in his hand and putting it back down on the bed.

He and Andrea were naked. They had fucked and were basking in the glow when she produced the box. He sat on the bed cross-legged, his recently spent cock coiled between his legs.

'It belonged to Max Ruga's second wife.'

'The one who died?'

'Yes. It is going to be very important to me. To the both of us. I need you to do me a very special favour. I want you to help me out here, okay?'

He nodded sheepishly.

Chapter Fifteen

IN HER MIND Andrea replayed her conversation with Philip. They had stayed in The Brink for over an hour and a half. For the past five days, she had been thinking things over. She was ready for Ruga.

The gallery was in Chelsea, off the Kings Road. Andrea made her way through the leafy street, glancing in antique shops. According to Philip, Ruga would arrive alone at eight-thirty precisely. He would not be early or late, Philip told her. Of that she could be sure. And he would most definitely be alone. Ruga liked to be alone with Rothko.

Andrea had done some reading on Rothko. She dipped into several books on him and went to see some of the paintings at the Tate. Rectangular colour fields stacked on top of each other on the canvas, starting bright early in his life and getting darker prior to his suicide. One quote said that some people broke down and wept in front of them, such was the power of the experience. Andrea found them expressive, and at an unconscious level unsettling, as though they were tapping into some low level co-ordinates and manipulating them. She called Philip to check precisely which period the Rothkos in the gallery would be from. The Black Paintings, he told her. The ones he started in his last year.

On a cool afternoon in late spring, Chelsea could not have seemed brighter. Andrea turned into the side street, swinging her overnight bag at her side. She came to the building which had a number only, no name to indicate a gallery would be hidden away inside. She pushed the single button on the entry phone.

'Yes,' a voice crackled.

'My name's Andrea King. I'm here from Philip.'

The door buzzed and she pushed it. The man she assumed to be the gallery owner was waiting behind the door. She did not expect him to be there so soon and he startled her. He was in his fifties, overweight and wearing an ill-fitting two piece suit with no tie. His shirt collar flapped and grey chest hairs sprouted from the top of his shirt. He was balding and the skin of his jowls hung loosely. His moustache looked oily. He eyed her up and down and she felt a shiver go up her spine.

'You'll be guiding Mr Ruga, I understand?' His accent was upper-class English.

'Yes, that's right.'

'Let me show you through to the gallery and I'll be off. Leave you to it.'

He led her down a small passageway and then opened a heavy wooden door. He showed her into the gallery.

'There will only be security here tonight, no one else. It is one guard. He will see Mr Ruga in and let the both of you out. He is under the strictest instructions not to disturb you. The very strictest,' he finished, looking at the bag in Andrea's hand

and then at her crotch in a less than subtle way.

'Thank you,' she said, smiling at him.

He handed her a key.

'It locks from either side,' he said, by way of explanation. 'My regards to Philip when you see him.'

With that he was gone.

Andrea locked the large door and left the key turned in it. Alone, she took in the room for the first time. It was a perfect square, perhaps forty feet by forty feet. Walls, floor and even ceiling seemed to be made of stone. There was a chill atmosphere familiar from many art galleries she had visited. No natural light entered the room. The only concession to an outside world were the grilles for the air conditioning. It was like a vault. Like a diamond robbery, she thought to herself, recalling Philip's words.

A bench was in the centre of the room. It was in the exact centre. About eight feet long and four feet wide, it was set in a small pit with a few steps leading down to it. It looked like a sunken Japanese garden, the way the bench was lower than the rest of the room by a foot or two.

On each wall, a Rothko painting. She looked at each of the four in turn. Black rectangle on grey rectangle. They looked impassively down from the walls, taking in all the light around them. Spots were carefully positioned to give the maximum effect. As she looked at each in turn, the silence in the room seemed to intensify. The paintings were so simple. Two colours. The top half of the canvas one dark colour, the bottom half not so dark. Yet it was this simplicity that was fascinating. It held her.

She reached a precise distance from one of the canvases and knew instinctively it was the place at which to stop. For a few minutes, she looked at each of the four in turn, familiarising herself. Then, not wanting to be late, she went to the bench in the middle of the room and opened her bag. She went and stood on the bench, in its centre, and found that it was a perfect vantage point from which to view the canvases, taking a different one in with each turn.

She removed all of her clothes, folding them carefully and placing them in a carrier bag. The floor was cold under her feet. She stretched herself and shrugged her shoulders slowly and continuously, feeling the muscles loosen. The bag contained various accoutrements she would need and now she removed from it a black Lycra one-piece body-suit. It was skintight. She pulled it over her legs and left it around her waist, leaving the top half down.

From the bag, she removed a body harness. It was not unlike the skeleton of a waistcoat made from leather straps held together by metal rings. Placing her arms into it like a jacket, she pulled it tight around her front and fastened it. The straps made an outline for her ribcage and breasts, lifting them up proudly. She pulled up the suit and put her arms through the vest-like top half. The harness showed through and her breasts lifted and pushed out against the shiny black material. Her nipples were like points in the fabric.

No shoes or long gloves to cover her exposed feet and arms. She had queried Philip about this detail and he had been emphatic. Definitely no shoes or gloves. Just the minimum. The body harness and the body-suit. She delved into the holdall and removed the box Philip had given to her along with a riding crop that was lying along the bottom of the bag, curving slightly as it was too long for it. She checked in the bag to make sure she had everything else there.

While she waited, she thought about the last weeks. DRA, Tim, the MCC course, the job, Ruga and the Onyx re-launch, Martin and Gillian. All of these things were converging and she was managing the situation with care. She would draw the diverse elements together. In the cool silence of the gallery, overlooked by the paintings, she drifted into a state of relaxation that was almost trance-like. The wait relaxed her completely and she did not even check her watch, which she had positioned on the top of the bag.

When she did look at the watch, it was eight twenty-five. She went and unlocked the door, leaving the key in the lock, then she sat on the narrow end of the bench with her back to the door. Behind her, on the granite of the bench, was the box. In front of that, the black leather riding crop. This would be Ruga's view as he entered the room. Andrea dressed in black, body harness lifting her breasts, sitting with her back to him. Behind her, in his field of vision would be a box and the crop.

Andrea reached into her bag and pulled out the blindfold. She placed it over her eyes, pulling it tight. The low light of the room was shut out. She placed her hands out at her sides, gripping the bench. Waiting. Her breathing sounded loud and she consciously moderated it to a low and steady rhythm. The blackness before her eyes was like journeying to the centre of one of the four paintings that looked down on her and surrounded her. Cologne and the faintest trace of manly perspiration. She felt their presence even with the blindfold on.

The door handle moved. The door opened, creaking slightly and then closed again. The key turned in the lock. Silence. One word, muttered under the breath and in an accent that was thick.

'Clara?' A hoarse questioning to the voice.

Footsteps on the stone floor. They came round her side and then she could hear him in front of her. His breath was rapid and confused. He gave a small sigh. As though he were holding his breath, all noise in the room stopped. Andrea sat on the granite bench and waited. She tired her hardest to remain expressionless, keeping her jawline solid. This was the crucial moment. What Ruga decided to do next would be of critical importance. He could easily flee the room and she would never see him. She waited.

She heard him remove clothing. It was difficult to tell what was being removed and in what order. His bare feet padded and went down the three steps. He was standing in front of her. She could smell him, a sweet smell. She felt his hands reach behind, loosen the blindfold and remove it.

Even the subdued light of the gallery flooded her retinas. She blinked several times and looked up at Max Ruga. In him she saw his son Max and his daughter Maxine. Ruga's skin was olive like his son's. The eyebrows were the characteristic heavy-set of son and daughter. The eyes themselves shone out, the brightest thing in the room. It was a slightly older version of the man she had seen in the photographs, but essentially the same. He was naked and as he stood while she sat, so his crotch was level with her face. For a man in his late fifties, his body was incredibly well preserved. It was how Philip would look in another ten years. She compared it mentally to the specimen that had let her in earlier.

He reached out and cradled her head, his hands through her hair, then gently turned her face up to look at her. Now he smiled down at her and nodded silently, as though approving what he saw. He looked almost choked, tears welling in the shining eyes. With no words he walked behind her and she heard him climb on to the bench.

Andrea waited a few seconds, then stood and turned. Ruga was kneeling on all fours, his head down and his rear high. She picked up the riding crop, feeling the lightness of it in her hand. She stroked it over his buttocks, tickling the end of it further down and on under to where his balls dangled. She ran the tip up the crack of his rear and down again. She made circular motions around a small area of his right cheek. Andrea raised the crop and held it over her shoulder. It stayed there. Letting him wait and wonder, she did not bring her arm down immediately.

It made contact with Ruga and the sound was harsh in the small space of the gallery. He made no sound at all. After another pause, she lashed at him again, catching him square on the buttocks. Back, pause and down again. By the eighth or ninth time, she could feel her shoulder muscle start to ache and was conscious of the heavy and fast movements of her arm. When she had reached twelve and his cheeks had red lines on them, she stopped.

'Again. Please,' he implored her.

Another six strikes and she heard the breath escape from his body, the pain beginning to reach him. For the final six strokes, she concentrated on the same area, trying to make identical contact each time she flailed him with the crop. By the time she had administered the last stroke, her pussy was moist against the leotard, her pubic hair almost buzzing static. His buttocks were crimson in the area she had concentrated the latter part of his beating.

Ruga turned and sat on the bench with his feet on the floor. He winced slightly but then appeared grateful for the coolness of the stone beneath him. His cock was lithe and Andrea was keen to get to it before it became hard. She admired his self-control for resisting an erection while she whipped him. She retrieved a small silver cock ring from her bag. It was just over an inch in diameter. Nicely constricting, as Tim had discovered. She slid it over his shaft first. When it was at the end, resting on his scrotum, she held the ring close to him and pulled his testicles through. The ring made his cock and ball sac stand away from his body and already Andrea saw the blood gushing into his cock only to be denied exit from it by the ring.

Andrea picked the crop back up and traced it along the edge of Ruga's shaft. His member flinched under the touch of the leather. It feathered against him, tracing over his skin and causing friction. She tickled the tip of his cock and his glans. Gradually, his member became stiffer. The pressure of the cock ring made the veins stand out. He looked down at himself and then up at her. She felt the constriction of the harness around her own body. His cock was fully erect, pushing against the silver band, the sides of the shaft looking bloated.

Going down on her knees, she took him into her mouth. It was hot and already the early traces of lubricant filmed the head of his penis. He sighed and she felt the riding crop against the back of her neck. Ruga had one hand on each end and was using it to pull her head down on to him. She pulled away from him and as she did, he pulled hard on the crop. As she was forced back down on to his cock, she narrowed her mouth and felt it graze over her lips. Smoothing her mouth over him, she could see the silver loop that was holding him in check and making his cock swell so vastly. Her jaw ached from the width she had to keep her mouth open to accommodate him. His tug on the crop was harsh and she was careful to time her movements to maximise the sensation for him.

In an instant, the crop was gone from the back of her neck. He lifted her head from his cock and she looked up at him as the lines in his face shaped themselves into a modest smile.

'Stand. Please,' he said to her.

She did so, letting her body stand proudly, filling the body-suit and letting it cover her like a second skin.

He cupped her pussy in his hand. She felt his palm under her and she ached. He moved his hand in a slow and definite beat, barely moving her mound. The Lycra was warm and around her pussy she felt it move in time with Ruga's hand. He did not enter her or touch her clitoris. He simply let his palm undulate around her crotch as though he were afraid to wake it. Her juices trickled against the crotch of her suit, the material becoming damp from the touch of Max Ruga. While he cradled her in this way, she breathed slowly and let her eyes fix on one of the paintings. What she saw and what she felt blended into a single feeling that clutched her. Her vision blurred and the dark colours of the canvas ran into each other.

When he probed into her, only a fraction, with

his middle finger, she tensed around it. The material was coarse against her lips and it made them itch in a way she could hardly control. She reached out and placed her hand on his shoulders to steady herself, her eyes still fixed on a point over his shoulder as he sat on the edge of the stone bench. He masturbated her with a deft and certain motion, his finger pushing into her and the fabric of the body-suit stimulating her clitoris.

The material around her crotch stretched and gave under the movements of Ruga's hand. She could hear the sound the cloth made as it formed a barrier between his hand and her pussy. It was an insistent rubbing sound, hand scuffing material and material scratching pussy. Her clitoris was swollen beneath the sheath of black Lycra.

As she orgasmed, the painting and the black material seemed to swallow her. She retreated into a violent and secret darkness, her body straining against his fingers, against the hardness and against itself. She dug her nails into his bare shoulders and twisted her lower half, the orgasm destroying her composure. Flailing her head about, she felt the journey her orgasm made through her. Her inner thighs trembled and she felt the muscles ripple.

Her eyes were still closed when she felt the body-suit being peeled from her. As it came away, the freshness of the air in the room bathed her body. He worked it down until her top half was exposed, breasts lifted by the straps on the harness, and he brushed her nipples. She opened her eyes to look at him, then ran her hands in his hair, the soft mane of it. His hands were strong and they explored her breasts for a moment longer before they turned their attention to the leotard. It came down and was around her ankles. She stood before him, baring her naked pussy, so close to his face. She wanted to grab his face and push it in there, but she knew what would come next.

He asked her to lie on her back, then pushed her knees up to her chest. She clasped her hands together under the backs of her knees to keep her legs pushed against her chest. With a leather cord from her bag, he bound her wrists together and then tied the loose cord to the silver ring that joined the straps between her breasts. All the while, his cock was erect and looked about to explode, the ring at its base straining to hold him in check.

She struggled to lift her head and see him. He removed another item from her bag. It was a short fat rubber plug, the shape of an oval light bulb; thin at the end and broadening in the middle before tapering again to a thin end. Attached to its base was a tube that led to a small rubber bulb, like the pump on a perfume atomizer bottle.

He opened a jar of syrupy lubricant and dipped the plug into it. When it came out, it shone and glistened in the low lighting of the room. She let her head lie flat on the bench, legs pushed to her chest and wrists bound. He came to her and put the blindfold back on.

The tip of the plug touched her anus. In a second, it was inside of her. It pushed her muscles wide as the broad middle entered her and then she closed around its thin base. She opened her mouth so that he could insert the small rubber bulb. She bit down on to it and as she did so, the plug in her anus expanded slightly. It swelled inside her and pushed the muscles of her anus a fraction wider. He moved the plug about to ensure it was seated in her properly.

She heard the riding crop before she felt it. It made a whistling sound as it travelled through the air. When it contacted with her stretched buttocks, it made a cracking sound that surprised her. For a second or two she felt nothing, as though in shock. Then the sting from it hit her. She clenched her buttocks in response and bit down on the bulb in her mouth. As she did, the plug widened her anus further.

With each stroke, she clenched her buttocks more and bit down harder on the bulb. It was an efficient and cruel mechanism of pain and pleasure. At each stroke she became more careful in the way she timed the clenching of her anus with the bite of her teeth. The crop stung and it was that which started the chain. As her buttocks became warmer, so her anus was expanded around the plug which grew inside her. Her legs strained from their position against her chest and the bindings on her wrists were tight, restricting her movements. In all of this, the severest punishment of all was that her clitoris, crying out to be touched, was ignored. She wondered which would give first, if the plug would be at its maximum before he had finished beating her with the crop.

He removed the bulb from her mouth. Her jaw ached and her mouth felt empty without it. Her buttocks simmered. She hissed through clenched teeth as the plug expanded, the sound of his hand working the pressure. Her anus opened and she felt completely helpless. She struggled to regulate her breaths and slowly she accommodated the expansion. He untied her hands and removed the blindfold and she let her feet rest on the bench and adjusted her eyes to the light.

With no further use for it, Andrea removed the plug from her anus, feeling it pull on her as it left, moving her muscles in an unfamiliar direction and sending a strong feeling through her. She looked around at the paintings, the light in the room seeming darker, as though they had absorbed it all. In the squareness of the stone room, she felt surrounded by the canvases, as though together they had some sort of power that was over and above their separate qualities. They intensified the experience and tapped into her in a way that unsettled and excited her.

In the first suggesiton of intimacy, he leaned next to her and smoothed her hair, then kissed her on the mouth, gently and carefully as though he had known her for many years. At that moment, she supposed, he probably felt as though he had. As they embraced, she freed an arm and dipped her finger into the jar, covering them in the oily golden liquid. Generously, she worked her fingers into her rear, feeling its pliability and the readiness the plug had left in its wake.

She knelt on the bench, her face almost level with the box. The riding crop was discarded further up the bench. He kissed the cheeks of her behind.

'Open the box, please,' he whispered.

Manoeuvring on her elbows, Andrea lifted the lid of the box.

There, lying cold and hard on the soft velvet of the box's interior was a penis made from onyx. It looked similar to Ruga's own member, but not exactly the same. It even reminded her of his son's penis, with which she had become so familiar on that afternoon in Nice. It was of a similar design to the plug that she had just removed, a full-sized cock but at its base it tapered to half an inch in diameter before two largy onyx balls bulged from the end.

It was as Philip had described. The whole bizarre ritual had played down to the last detail. Now she was faced with the strangest family heirloom she could imagine. A crafted onyx penis, rumoured to be modelled on all manner of historical figures. Andrea knew instinctively that it was from the Rugas.

As Ruga removed the onyx phallus from its case, she let her eyes follow it, a quiver going through her. She closed her eyes and waited for him to introduce it into her rear. The plug had prepared her and the feeling was not one of pain. It was one of precision. Of penetration and completeness. The onyx was cold and it made her behind feel all the warmer. Andrea did not gasp as it filled her, merely drawing in a deep and almost silent breath as she felt the history of the Ruga men bear into her.

Her anus closed around the narrow section of the shaft above the balls. She felt the large spheres rest against the cheeks of her behind. Ruga spread her buttocks slightly to push the phalus and then closed them, her cheeks now clenching the balls.

With no words, Ruga cleared the stone bench and lay down on his back, his own penis standing high against the pressure of the cock ring. An animal craving gripped Andrea and she quickly squatted over him. She stayed in position, relishing the fullness of her rear and the emptiness of her vagina. It excited her, to know it was about to be penetrated. She moved her feet wider and let herself sink towards him.

The tip of his cock touched her lips. She was

utterly drenched in her own juices and his cock was rigid. She crouched over him and let the tip stay where it was, anticipating the severe ingress.

'Oh!'

She could not help herself. It felt so exact. So wide and so long. His phallus was at the opening of her vagina and she fed it into her. This man whom she had been chasing for what seemed like ages was now underneath her and entering her with a vengeance. A tingle ran up her spine and fizzled over to the right side of her head. His muscle entered further. She felt the ring at the base of his cock touch the outer lips of her pussy. He was inside her.

For a moment, she sat there. She ran her hands through her hair and then pulled at the straps of the body harness. They tightened under her breasts, lifting them in the air, making them distend. The cheeks of her rear were still heated from the flogging he had administered earlier. All the time, Ruga was studying her face, his hands resting lightly on her hips.

His cock was embedded deep in her pussy. She put her hands on his chest and moved her pussy over his cock. As she did so, the phallus pushed gently on her anus, its balls resting against Ruga's own.

Each time she reared up and away from his body, she felt his cock move out of her and the onyx in her behind. She felt full. With Ruga and with the onyx cock. As she moved over his single intrusion into her, she felt the invasion in her anus shift and move. She found a rhythm and depth that pulled and pushed on her in a pleasurable manner. With each raising of her body, she let only an inch or so of his cock in and out of her.

She shifted herself around on top of his prostrate form, unwilling to move too far away. She leaned her body more forward on to his, changing the angle of his shaft. She gasped.

Taking her by surprise, Ruga yanked hard and the dildo came several inches out of her. It made a short and raw journey from her anus and she welcomed the change in feeling it gave. It felt, momentarily, more like being fucked in both entrances at the one time.

'Ah!'

He had jerked it further from her. Her anus throbbed from its passing. Her breathing deepening, she started to drive herself more forcefully on to his cock. When he harshly pushed it back into her, she grunted and bucked on to him.

She lifted herself almost clear of his cock, raising herself up and returning to her squatting position, her feet planted either side of him and the stone bench rough under her soles. She began moving rhythmically, allow herself to elevate herself almost to the tip of his cock with each lunge. He sighed as she teemed around his cock with herself, letting him wallow in her depths.

Ruga lifted his shoulders off the bench, several times in short succession. Andrea recognised that his orgasm was approaching. She braced herself and flexed her vagina around him. She dropped herself down on his shaft and felt the hot metal of the cock ring that had constricted his orgasm for so long. It would burst from him soon in spite of the ring.

He cried out and she felt his cock swell. As the first surge of his semen spurted from him, Andrea began to stand upright. He shouted and convulsed, as though he were being dragged along the stone bench. His cock was out of her now and his own hand pumped at it. The come erupted from him and splattered on his stomach and chest. The bursts were heated and short, only the smallest traces of his spunk unloading at a time because of the squeeze of the cock ring. His whole body was a spasm and she continued to rise up on her legs. Andrea towered over him, the onyx cock hanging from her.

She masturbated herself furiously, her fingers commanding her clitoris to provide a quick release. She could barely hold her orgasm in and yet she had to be rough with herself to tip it out of her. She bent her knees and opened them wide, her hand a blur between her legs. She heaved and her shoulders fell forwards as she sumberged into the orgasm. It drowned her. She came hard and as she did so, she felt the rough jabs of Ruga, the phallus continuing to fuck her rear as she brought herself to the end. She called out in the silence of the gallery, her anus overloaded with feeling, her pussy lost in the paroxysm of her orgasm.

As her vision cleared, she looked down at Ruga. It was like awakening from a dream and suddenly having a sense of where she was. Sweat covered his body and as she looked closely at his face, she saw there, mixed with the perspiration, tears.

Chapter Sixteen

SHE WAS EXHAUSTED. It was one-thirty in the morning. In the quiet of her flat, her mind and body were still reeling from Max Ruga. Things had gone well. Very well indeed. It would be at least a week until things worked themselves through, but she was certain they would. They had already talked about her going back to Nice the next weekend. She may even take Tim, she thought to herself.

Tim.

She went to the kitchen and brought it to life with the low level fluorescents nestled above the work surfaces. As they flickered on she looked at the breakfast bar in the centre of the room for what she wanted.

It was there.

On top of the bar was a video cassette. On top of that, she saw, was a calling card Tim had left and on to which he had drawn a silhouette caricature of himself standing legs astride, hair sprouting. On the card he had written, 'And all because the lady loves . . .?' She smiled.

Next to the cassette was a small box of chocolates, silver cardboard wrapped with a pink ribbon. The kitchen was still and silent. She sighed, heard herself and thought how loud it sounded. She gathered the cassette and the chocolates and went to the living-room to check the tape.

She watched the tape in the silence of the dark room. It was fine. She ate one of the chocolates, a white praline, and went upstairs to find Tim.

He was in the bedroom asleep. The bedside lamp was on. It shone on his forehead and highlighted his nose, which twitched occasionally as he slept, as though he were doing long division in his head or choosing what to order from a menu. His arms were outside the bedclothes and the duvet was tucked tightly under them, revealing his shoulders. He had changed the bedclothes and the oatmeal linen of the duvet looked inviting. So did he. She imagined his naked body under the covers. She needed to shower.

Using the second bathroom rather than the en suite, so as not to wake Tim, she quickly removed her makeup. In no time, she was out of her clothes. Her body still felt constricted and marked by the uniform she had worn earlier, at the gallery, and ached from the uses it had been put to by Ruga. Her breasts felt heavy and her jaw was numb. The weals on her behind had subsided, cooling into small red marks she examined in the mirror. Between her legs, her pussy felt as though it were yawning. Her anus had a strained feeling.

All of these feelings she washed away under the shower water, using its cascade to soothe her body and purge her mind. She turned the water up fast and hot and smeared shower gel all over herself. She had forgotten there was a bottle of

Chanel shower gel in this bathroom and she enjoyed the luxuriant feel and delicate fragrance of it all over her body. She stood longer than normal under the powerful stream, letting it flood over her. The suds gathered and swirled into a whirlpool as they disappeared. Afterwards she patted at her body with a bath towel, then moisturised it all over her body eagerly drinking in the fluid. Soon her skin was warm and pliable. Naked, she padded along the hallway to the bedroom.

He was still sleeping. He had moved on to his side, facing the side of the bed. Carefully, she slipped under the covers. The fresh, comforting feel of the linen touched her everywhere. She stretched her legs and moved closer to Tim's back. She came to rest against him and fitted her body around the shape of his. She pressed her groin into his rear and raised her knees so that the fronts of her legs were on the back of his. She put an arm around him and he, still asleep, pulled it into his chest, murmuring as he did so.

Her body pressed against Tim's, she held the pose. The arm she had round him rose and fell in time with his even breaths. Her own breath expanded her against his back. Gradually, their respiration synchronised. She held him tightly and looked at the lightly tanned skin on the back of his neck. A warm rush went through her.

She allowed her hand to travel over the muscle of his chest and on to his stomach. The skin was velvety and she found his navel, where it protruded, and she ran a finger around it, listening all the time to sounds of his breathing, his chest rising and falling in the steady rhythm of sleep. His pubic hair was bristly and she pushed her fingers into its thatch, finding the soft mound of skin that lay beneath. She crept her finger through until she came to the base of his cock, then pushed her fingers into the base, feeling its sinewy and muscular quality. Across the top she traced a finger. His cock was warm and the skin sheathing the muscle was thick and lush. She held it in her hand and it slumbered almost as soundly as Tim. She would wake it up. Before she woke Tim, she would rouse his cock.

For several minutes she lay holding Tim's cock. She carefully squeezed it, feeling the way it shuddered as she did so. The outside edge of her little finger rested against his ball sac while the rest of her fingers closed around his cock. It grew in her hand. At first the change in width and length was almost equal. As it pushed out of her fingers, so it also extended through them. She pushed herself against his rear feeling her pussy awaken. His buttocks were tight and she raised one leg to let it lie on his hip, opening her pussy a fraction. As he flourished in her hand, she continued to squeeze him, counting a full second between each grip.

When he was fully erect in her hand, his breathing more irregular, she moved her hand up and down him. She played her fingertips over the head, tickling the glans underneath. With a sigh, he was awake. She could tell by the movements of his shoulders that he was no longer asleep. He did not turn around immediately, and she continued to stroke his cock, feeling it jump and move about in her hand. Now he turned to face her. She released him then closed her hand back around him, pulling him in.

'Hello,' he said.

'Hello, you,' she said. She kissed him.

'How did it go?' He was still half-asleep, hair tousled.

'Very well. I'll tell you about it tomorrow. After the last module of the course. Thanks for getting the video, by the way.'

'It's the right one, then?'

'Oh yes, it's the right one. Don't tell me you didn't look at it?'

'I might have,' he smiled.

'And thank you for the chocolates.'

She disappeared under the quilt and took his cock in her mouth. It was dark under the linen covers. She opened her mouth wide and covered him with it, and he gasped at the suddenness of her movement. Moving her head around in a circular motion, she let the apex of his cock roll about inside her mouth, then she lowered her head further and took more of him into her mouth. Now she rested her hands on the mattress, either side of him, and brought his cock up at a straight angle, pointing it away from his body. She positioned her head so that she was directly above his crotch, his cock pointing directly into her mouth, paused for a second and then swiftly dropped her head, the cock going deep into her mouth and on to the back of her throat. She relaxed her throat muscles as much as she could and held her position.

'Oh God!' she heard him call from up above the covers, his hands banging on the mattress and echoing under the tent of the duvet cover.

She suckled on him, pulling him into her mouth by drawing at his shaft, her cheeks sucked in a concave from the pressure. She placed her hands on the front of his hipbones and lazily moved her mouth up and down. Her spittle spread over him and the lubricating effect made her movements more slick and fluid. As she sheathed him with her mouth, his cock urged sturdily outwards. She could feel the shape of his head, the spread of his phallus as her head rose. She did not let the head of his cock slip from her mouth. Instead, when she felt the hard ridge of his phallus against the insides of her lips, she used it as a guide for when to stop and go down in the opposite direction.

The bedclothes were warm around her and sounded crisp as they moved in time with her. Tim had raised the covers with his hands and she felt cool fresh air filter into the enclosed space. The light also seeped in and she looked at his stomach, the line of hair that began at his navel and traced into the brush of brown pubic hair. When his cock was almost out of her mouth, she could see its root, the source from which it had grown with her earlier encouragements, the source from which she could, in any number of ways, cause an eruption.

With her tongue, she tapped at the peak of his cock while it was still in her mouth. The top of her tongue found the eye and she tasted him, letting her tongue undulate beneath, as though she were repeatedly poking out her tongue. He shifted himself and she felt his legs go tense. Having him come in her mouth would have been nice. To smother him and plug off his orgasm as it happened from deep within him and on into the confines of her mouth was an exciting thought. But she felt the need for him to penetrate her. She wanted to feel him pry her open and slide into her. The sensation of his shaft against the walls of her vagina. She wanted to ride him, feel the stiff rod ramming into her soft and wet pussy, a combination of hard and soft, pleasure and pain, desire and release.

She let him slip from her mouth and placed

kisses all over his abdomen. Then she knelt upright and threw the cover fully back, gazing at his nude body against the oatmeal, his gold skin radiant, his cock fully erect and his eyes burning a slow passion for her. Desperately she dropped her head to his chest, nuzzling at his nipples and running her tongue around one. She put her hand down and felt his balls, small and hard, his body greedily pulling them into himself. Squeezing them in her hand she pulled them away from his body, then bent and opened her mouth wide, taking one gently inside. The skin of his ball sac was squeezed in her mouth and the testicle was hot. The hairs from his sac tickled her tongue. Gently and cautiously, she sucked, gradually increasing the pressure. He yelped as she did so and his hands grabbed at her head. She let the ball drop from her mouth and watched it retreat, the skin wrinkling as it did so.

Now Tim sat up on the bed, supporting himself with his hands on the mattress as she sat astride him, her knees wide. The tops of his legs felt muscular and fiery beneath her. They eyed each other and their mouths found each other, lips making familiar and exciting patterns on each other. She raked her nails along his sides and he pushed himself off his hands and gripped her tightly, face buried between her breasts. She looked down at the flop of hair and stroked it, feeling him breathe and feeling the beat of her heart. Blood flowed wildly through her body, coursing into every region and enlivening her. Down deep, her pussy was deliriously filled with the rush and steeped in juices of its own.

She held the sides of his face while he sucked at her nipple. Its tip was long and distended and with his tongue he moved it from side to side. It was so erect she felt as though it would sway under its own weight were Tim not there. The movement of his lips over the tip of her tit were not unlike the earlier ones she had made over his cock. Zones all over her body were crying out for attention and she sighed, holding him close and biding her time. She closed her eyes and let her head fall limply backwards.

Tim's hand was stroking one of the cheeks of her backside. His fingers made small circular motions over it and it made her acutely aware of the sensitivity of her skin. He cupped the whole buttock and squeezed it, his grip firm. With all the fingers of the hand, he stroked the crack of her rear, never venturing in, only along. The caress continued, from the base of her back down to her perinaeum. The touch was so light she could barely feel the weight of the hand that did it. Perhaps by a millimetre at a time, his fingers neared her pussy. Each time his fingers came downwards, she felt her stomach flutter, as though she were about to hurtle down on a rollercoaster. She drew her breath in sharply every time he came close to her pussy, the finger agonizingly close, but not close enough.

Gradually, his fingers began to explore the outer reaches of her pussy, rubbing lightly on its borders. Casually they lighted against her lips which pouted and trembled at the brush. It was no heavier than the feeling of a feather, stroking against her, but what such a deft and delicate motion threatened was a powerful torrent of emotion, sex and passion. She moaned and fluffed the hair on the back of his head. Moving closer to him she brought her legs around him, the backs of her calves touching the small of his back. Her pussy dropped low and spread open.

She felt it there, suspended above the linen sheet, gaping and ready.

Tim's fingers moulded expertly into the folds of her lips. He moved them around and then spread them for a moment. Without further caution, he massaged her clitoris deeply, sending pulsations through the whole of her groin area. Her clitoris felt as though it had taken on a life of its own. She buried her head into Tim's shoulder and in her mind's eye imagined her clitoris, erect in its folds of skin. She opened her mouth and took a small bite at his shoulder, rolling the skin between her teeth.

His cock must have been held away from her by his arm since when he removed his hand from her pussy, she felt his member spring up against the inside of her thigh. It made a faint slapping noise and was solid and insistent against her. She wanted to feel more than just its weight against her pussy. She released him from the grip of her legs and pushed his shoulders until he was lying on his back, his cock now settled between her legs as she sat astride him. She shook her hair, still slightly damp from the shower, and caressed his torso, feeling his whole body beneath her – his firm masculine body, brimming and throbbing with life.

As he had teased her with his fingers, now it was her turn to tease him. She used her pussy to do it. Shifting her position, she retrieved him from between her legs and gripped his cock. She ran the point of it along her moist lips. Fluid met fluid; his and hers. The lips of her pussy were full and the end of his cock perfect, sliding so readily into her. She rubbed the top of his cock at her clitoris, enjoying the way he jumped about in her hands, his hands covering his face as he quivered up and down the slit. She toyed with him, exactly the same as he had done to her. When she thought he could take it no longer, she did it more. He groaned and jerked.

In a fluid and practised movement, she positioned his cock at the opening of her vagina and sank on to it, mirroring the familiar and rehearsed procedure she had earlier performed on him with her mouth. She did it in a deliberate and steady way, giving her a precise feeling of being penetrated by him. Her pussy almost gulped him up. She swallowed him far inside of herself, the feeling of his cock rigid and incisive, parting her and widening her. She squeezed her muscles around him. He removed his hands from his face and the grimace was replaced by a much more beatific smile. He stretched his hands out and took her breasts in them, shaping soft palms around them. Then his hand, a thumb to be precise, found her clitoris and pressed at it, as though it were a button that would start her.

She clenched herself. Everything. Her teeth. Her muscles. Her pussy. Her bottom. She felt everything in her pull together and compose. After the power of this hold on his body had exercised itself, she relaxed herself and released him. The only point of tension that remained in her was coming from outside of her. Tim's cock was like a stone inside her. It could have been made of marble, or onyx, she thought; it was a perfect stillness and rigidity around which she would move. She looked at him, lying on the pillow, his fine features flattered by the light. She thought of all the things that had first attracted her to him. They came back, flowing into her mind and flooding it. The feelings were all compounded into a single powerful need. She wanted to be fucked. Not just to be fucked. To be fucked by him.

The distance, she supposed, was not in real terms that great. The movement of her over him. His cock inside her. It was simple and straightforward and yet it brought on feelings so intense and so complex. She travelled the length of his cock with her vagina at a speed that was no faster then her steady, deep breaths. She drove his cock into her with all the control she could muster. Their bodies made a sleek and slippery sound as they contacted with each other. Her pussy was like a well-oiled machine completing a precision process. After her earlier exertions with Max Ruga, she was grateful to fall into a safe and uncomplicated pattern.

Beneath her, Tim stared up. She tried to read his mind, wondered what was going through it at that moment. She held his gaze and jerked herself down slightly harder and with an edge more of aggression, her rear banging into him. As though she were being mesmerised, her eyelids became heavy. They fluttered and she closed them. All that was left was him inside her.

Their bodies and their minds moved closer to a joint abandon. Both ready to relinquish their grip and allow passion to rupture the thin, charged veil of sex between them. It would burst through in a torrent, carrying the both of them along. Tim moved himself about, burrowing his cock in deeper and she met his movements with equal enthusiasm, her pussy animated and alive.

She pressed on her clitoris, crying out as she did so, the first slow and yearning throb of an orgasm quaking in her. She was not ready for the jolt. She held herself on the edge of it, concentrating her mind and controlling her feelings. She kept her eyes closed and teetered on his cock as though on a high wire. She moved just enough to bring him off, all the while continuing to massage herself, ready to follow him over the edge.

One hand pressed on his stomach, the other on her clitoris. Still she would not speed up her movements. Tim had all but given up and was ready to erupt, sending a barrage of his come into her. She could sense it there in him, waiting to release. It filled him and unbalanced him. When he let it go into her, she knew part of him would go with it. She had held him within herself and was coaxing his fluid from him. She imagined his cock, up inside of her, the way the head would expand as it pumped into her. She thought of the feelings that would go through his body, the force at which he would discharge himself.

Tim cried out. He was helpless. He was no longer in control of himself or his body. She opened her eyes to see him. His body was a taut contortion, shoulders straining and lips stretched over his teeth. She shivered and shifted barely an inch up and down on him. He shouted her name and steadied his convulsions by holding her hips. She watched him try and resist his own movement, to hold on to his orgasm for as long as possible. It was too late. It was already hers.

With his cock still jerking involuntarily inside her, his semen inside her, she worked away at her clitoris. Her whole body was taken over. In her groin and stomach, a buzz spread. It went down her legs, all the way to the tips of her toes. It rose up, across her chest and out over her shoulders. Her arms slackened and she became fluid. She felt as though she had metamorphosised. From skin through to a shimmering compound and finally on into water. She felt completely and utterly free and flowing – her body was a wave, able to move and experience pleasure in any way she chose. In the moment, she lost herself an felt as though she were being remade. As she came in spasms, her pussy in a tumult, she felt reconstituted and whole again, but touched by the experience. She looked at Tim as though it was the first time she had ever seen him.

'Oh Andrea . . .'

She put a finger over his lips, smothering the words.

Chapter Seventeen

ANDREA AWOKE FROM a sleep that had, to her knowledge, been deep and free from dreams or anxiety. It was six forty-five. Six forty-four to be precise. One minute before her alarm was due to go off. She left Tim sleeping, having spent a few moments holding his dormant form, taking in his body heat.

MCC3. The final module. It would not have been out of the ordinary at any other time. For everyone else who would be there this morning, it would be nothing special. They did not know what she knew. MCC3. Anderson. The two words meshed like gears in her mind and set her into routine.

She showered quickly, part-fresh from her shower last night, part-sullied from the sex that followed it. She sat in her robe, her hair tied back, and looked at herself in the mirror. Today needed to be special. All over. From the ground up.

She applied Chanel liquid foundation. Staying in the same vein, she opened the black lacquered box and dusted her large brush into it and then on to her face. Eyes were all Lancôme – liner, shadow and mascara. She outlined her lips with

Paloma Picasso and then filled it in with a red that was almost fire-engine. With practised care, she fixed her hair, shaping it and enjoying the way it hung. It was her most vain time of the day. She always enjoyed what she saw. And enjoyed the fact she enjoyed it. She sprayed a fine amount of Escape on, lingering in its scent for a few moments before going to the wardrobe.

La Perla underwear, retrieved from a hanger, began her ensemble. In her mind, she ran through alternatives, seeing each outfit on herself, the line of it, the impression it would create. It was not a casual day on MCC3. They would be doing some presentations that were filmed and appraised, so they had been briefed to look smart. Ralph Lauren. A simple dress, cut smart and formal without being overbearing. She had picked it up in Harvey Nichols two weeks earlier and hadn't been able to put it down again.

The phone at the side of the bed warbled discreetly. She sat down, picked it up and cradled it under her right shoulder, fiddling with an earring in her left ear as she did so.

'Hello.'

'You certainly have an effect with the Ruga men.'

It was Maxine.

'Hi. And the Ruga women, I hope.'

'Father asked me to contact you. He was very impressed. He would like to see you again. Did he mention this?'

'Yes. We talked about my coming to Nice, possibly this weekend. I think he would like some more time to consider things,' Andrea answered, the earring now inserted.

'He sounded quite certain when he called me. Animated almost. He said you had recaptured the spirit of what Onyx was always supposed to be. Congratulations.'

Maxine's voice sounded clear. Andrea wondered where she was calling from.

'Shall I take it that Nice is on?'

'Definitely.'

Andrea looked over her shoulder. 'I was thinking of bringing Tim with me. Would that be acceptable?'

'More than acceptable,' replied Maxine, a lascivious trace in her voice. 'Let me give you the number here and you can leave details of your flights. We'll send a car.'

Andrea noted the number on the writing pad on the bedside table. She checked the clock. Seven twenty-five.

'Maxine, I'm expecting someone right now. Let me call you later, okay?'

'Sure. Ciao.'

'Bye.'

Deanna arrived at seven-thirty as they had arranged.

'Very nice. Not too powerful, but an undertow,' said Deanna when she saw Andrea's outfit. 'You're going to knock them over today. Look at the rags I have to wear, but I'm just the help.'

They had a cup of coffee seated at the breakfast bar.

'Who are the chocolates from?' asked Deanna, eyeing the box suspiciously.

'They're from Tim. Isn't he a sweetheart?'

'A bit too much of a sweetheart if you ask me. Too much for you. I hope you're not going to break his little heart, And.'

'I don't plan on it. I like him. A lot. He's good to me.'

210

'Can I at least have a chocolate? That's as sexy as I get lately. Chocolate at seven-thirty in the morning.'

Deanna took a gold foil-wrapped concoction from the box and ran a nail under the wrapper.

'Are you sure Anderson will be at the hotel?' Andrea asked her.

'Of course. He was booked in there last night, after he arrived back from Munich. I knew you'd ask me that, so I called and checked with the desk. He's there.'

Deanna took a mouthful of coffee, seeming satisfied with the fact that she knew where Anderson was.

'Suppose he sees you at the hotel?'

'He won't. If he does, I'll say Leanne asked me to check something for her because she wasn't feeling well. He doesn't know who does what on these courses.' Deanna sipped more coffee at the last word of sentence, which was lost in the acoustics of the cup.

'And all the course materials are there already?'

'Don't worry, And.'

'I'm not worrying. I just like to know things are running smoothly.'

'Yes. The course materials are there. After that time last December when they got stopped at Dublin airport and didn't make it to Galway, we always have to have them in the night before. Wherever the course is held. They will have been delivered late last night. Anyway, do you have something for me?'

Andrea went to the living-room and returned with the tape.

'It's set up to run from the start?' asked Deanna.

'Yes. You'll just need to do a label for it.'

'No problem.'

211

She saw Deanna off at the door. They hugged silently.

'See you later,' Deanna said, smiling and clutching the tape.

Andrea ordered a taxi to pick her up at eight-fifteen. The ride would be only twenty minutes. She made conversation with the driver and tipped heavily, getting a receipt for expenses.

The Crayford Hotel, unlike the hotels for MCC1 and MCC2, was dignified rather then countrified. It had an endearingly Edwardian Merchant-Ivory bustle to it, as though a soundtrack were echoing around a high marble ceiling. She located the room on the welcome board, rather than trawling through her paperwork. She was loath to get the coursework papers out. She didn't imagine she would need them for very long.

People had already arrived. About eight in all. Another seven or so to follow, plus Martin and David Wheeler. And Carl Anderson. Andrea made small talk and gossiped with her assembled colleagues, careful about what she said about who, playing the usual game. She knew most of the people well enough to wander just far enough into dangerous territory without stepping on a land mine.

'Hello, Gill,' she said to Gillian Kay as she entered the room, looking like she was off for an interview as headmistress at a finishing school.

'Martin not come yet?'

'He's on his way,' Gillian said, forcing a polite smile.

'As ever, Gill. As ever.'

'Thank you by the way,' Andrea said.

'I'm sorry?' Gillian looked confused.

'Thank you for the congratulations.'

This time Gillian said nothing. She merely looked confused.

'The Lazzo account. We've won it. Client spend probably in the order of 1.5 million this year. I suppose we were both wrong on the forecast front.'

She walked away before Gillian could respond.

Carl Anderson entered the room behind Martin Cox and David Wheeler. The murmur in the room was audible from the rhythm it made. No words were discernible from anyone, but the message was subliminally transmitted – what was Anderson doing here?

'Carl has asked to be a part of the proceedings today,' David Wheeler announced cautiously, aware that he was answering a silent question going through every mind in the room. 'He's not here to observe anyone. He just wants to take a look at the course, see how things are going.'

Andrea marvelled at the way people spoke about Anderson as though he were not present, whether he was there or not. She supposed he would like to think of himself as always present. Not unlike a god. The room had the silence of prayer.

'We're going to launch right into it today,' said Martin, falling into a double act with David Wheeler for Anderson's benefit. 'We'll review the exercises to be done after we look at the first film. It follows the progression of our friend Mullins, the account handler we've been tracking through the last two modules. You'll see she's up against it in this clip. As we know, she is a very tenacious woman. I think we can all appreciate her predicament and learn something from it.'

He took the tape from the box and pushed it into the machine. It clicked into play mode automatically. David Wheeler lowered the lights and Martin made his way to his seat, next to Anderson. Martin looked pleased with himself. A job well done. Andrea saw him shoot a sidelong glance at Gillian who nodded approvingly.

The video hissed and the lead-in turned to a dark picture. It was a little fuzzy and difficult to make out at first. There was a time clock in the bottom right corner as though it was a rough cut of a video, except that it just showed a date and time the way a home video recorder would, not the fine fractions of a second a professional video would have.

Several people in the room looked confused, expecting to see the familiar surroundings and actors that had featured in the previous videos on modules one and two.

The picture cleared. A bright red Porsche. On its bonnet, a man was lying back across the sloping curve that led to the windscreen. He wore no trousers or underwear. A woman knelt and was fellating the man extremely quickly, like she was blowing up a life ring on the Titanic, Andrea thought.

Andrea felt the whole room very quickly establish three important facts.

The red Porsche belonged to Carl Anderson.

The man was Martin Cox.

The woman was Gillian Kay.

John, the security guard, had kept an eye out for the last two weeks. Andrea had been waiting, willing Martin to do the same old, tame old routine with Gillian on the bonnet of Anderson's car. When he did, John was ready. The security cameras in the building possessed a range of capabilities, most of which were not ordinarily used. John had run the camera at its normal speed instead of the stop motion they normally used. Better still, he had switched on the microphone.

'Oh baby, that's it. Suck Carl's big cock. Carl's got a big rod for you, you dirty bitch. Lick it, oh yeah.'

The room erupted at about the same time as Martin did on the video, jerking about on the bonnet of Anderson's Porsche. If he could have held on to his orgasm a little longer, Andrea thought, he might have salvaged some respect.

When Martin stood from his place next to Carl Anderson, Andrea thought he was about to try and turn the video off. She fingered the remote control that she had popped in her bag earlier, ready to start it again if he did.

He did not. He fled.

Several seconds later, with the cool and collected precision of a contract killer, Carl Anderson left the room.

Andrea turned and looked at Gillian Kay, who was ashen, her face the colour of day-old dough.

'I think we can all learn something from that,' Andrea smiled at her.

Chapter Eighteen

SEX. THAT WAS where it started and ended, Andrea thought to herself, resting her briefcase on Martin's old desk.

Most people who attended MCC3 that day – Martin Cox, Gillian Kay and Carl Anderson excluded – thought that the video was a good gag to pull, even if it was a bit near the knuckle. It was understandable that Martin would have fled the way he did. Gillian was seen as a good sport for remaining seated at least until the video was shut off. However, when Martin did not return to DRA at all, there was surprise. A rumour started that Anderson had killed him with a death grip or a flying kick. It was confusing and seemed a little harsh that Martin should be out of the door on such a weak pretext. Unlike Andrea, of course, these spectators did not have access to the stranger truth.

When she first hit on the idea of the security tape, it had been Andrea's intention to embarrass Martin and Gillian. She would raise a laugh at their expense and whatever fall-out damage it caused would have been a bonus. Then, two important facts had come to her attention.

Deanna had told her about Anderson attending the conference. As importantly, Carol had found out that Gillian was also having a fling with Anderson. That explained the extremity of Anderson's reaction.

Andrea had not, nor would she ever, reveal to Carl how the security video ended up where it did. He had no idea. Deanna had slipped in and out of the Crayford Hotel that morning unnoticed. There was no witch-hunt or post-mortem over the whole episode. It was handled swiftly. MCC3 went on that day, although Gillian Kay was apparently feeling unwell and therefore unable to attend the rest of the course.

Anderson fired Martin Cox over the telephone that same afternoon. According to Carl it had been a race to get the words out before Martin beat him to it by resigning. Andrea had since heard that Martin was thinking of forming an agency with Mike Mitchell, the Creative who resigned after the announcement of the new position at MCC2. If this was true, DRA would also certainly lose Deanna, who was still loyal to her old boss. Gillian Kay seemed determined to hang on at DRA for as long as Anderson's whim held.

The weekend following MCC3, Andrea went to Nice with Tim. Max Ruga senior was not there, but it did not matter. In between the various interesting combinations she, Tim and the Ruga siblings involved themselves in, Maxine and Andrea laid the business foundation for what followed in the next ten days. Things moved quickly. Within a week of the Nice weekend, Ruga and Anderson met. It took less than four days to secure the account. As a thank-you and congratulation, Max Ruga sent Andrea four Mark

Rothko prints. In the process, she got to work closely with Carl Anderson, coming to understand something of who he was and why he was that way. Anderson was very impressive indeed.

More importantly, he was very impressed with Andrea.

She had decided that Martin's old desk would have to go. That would be one of her two caprices. The other, she was about to resolve immediately and did not need a new desk to accomplish. These sorts of transactions could be carried out over a wallpaper pasting table.

She had been Creative Director of Deakin, Richards and Anderson for over a month now and had used Martin's office virtually unchanged apart from a few of her own personal touches. For her meeting this morning, she added one further, supplied by Tim. It was a small replica model of a red Porsche 911. She set it on the desk so that it just poked out from behind her small black clock. She hoped Gillian would catch sight of it while she was firing her. If Carl had any sentimentality left in his body, none of it was reserved for Gillian Kay. The whim had obviously floundered. When Andrea suggested it was time for new blood, Anderson had not hesitated in agreeing. 'Purge the old blood where you see fit,' he had said.

She glanced out of one of her windows, the familiar skyline of London greatly improved at this height. A plane crossed the panorama, bound for Heathrow, a white stream in its wake. She picked up her phone and pushed the button for her assistant. She turned her attention back to the plane, cutting through the air smoothly and silently, certain of where it was going.

'Julie, send for Gillian Kay.'

HOTEL APHRODISIA

Dorothy Starr

The luxury hotel of Bouvier Manor nestles near a spring whose mineral water is reputed to have powerful aphrodisiac qualities. Whether this is true or not, Dani Stratton, the hotel's feisty receptionist, finds concentrating on work rather tricky, particularly when the muscularly attractive Mitch is around.

And even as a mysterious consortium threatens to take over the Manor, staff and guests seem quite unable to control their insatiable thirsts . . .

0 7515 1287 7

AROUSING ANNA

Nina Sheridan

Anna had always assumed she was frigid. At least, that's
what her husband Paul had always told her – in between
telling her to keep still during their brief weekly fumblings
under the covers and playing the field himself during his
many business trips.

But one such trip provides the chance that Anna didn't
even know she was yearning for. Agreeing to put up a
lecturer who is visiting the university where she works, she
expects to be hosting a dry, elderly academic, and
certainly wasn't expecting a dashing young Frenchman
who immediately spoke to her innermost desires. And,
much to her delight and surprise, the vibrant Dominic
proves himself able and willing to apply himself to the
task of arousing Anna . . .

0 7515 1222 2